Whale Magic

Written by Karina Arana

This book is a work of fiction. The characters, incidents, and dialogue are drawn from the author's imagination and are not to be construed as real. Any resemblance to actual events, persons, or businesses are coincidental or used fictitiously.

No part of this book may be used or reproduced in any manner whatsoever without written permission except in the case of brief quotations embodied in critical articles and reviews. For more information address the author at crabbey@me.com.

Edited by Cristal Celine Murray

Designed and illustrated by Nikolas Arana

Written in San Jose del Cabo, Mexico in 2016, by Karina Arana
First edition May 2017

For my girlies, Madeleine, Sophia, Charlotte, Alexa, and Eva

Acknowledgements

Thank you to my Mom, Dad and Melina, who kept me afloat while I wrote. Thank you to Melina who first coined the term "whale magic". Thank you to Horacio and Melina for being our family's Baja pioneers.

Thank you to my first readers Mari, Stefanie, Michele, Jackie and Bert.

Thank you to Cristal for editing.

Thank you to Niko for the cover/illustrations.

Thank you to DJ for encouraging me to write and inspiring me to publish.

Thank you to all the students I've had the privilege of working with.

Thank you to all the activist heroes out there fighting the good fight for those who don't have a voice.

Mil gracias a la Baja, mi inspiración. Ojalá sea siempre querida, protegida y apreciada.

Chapter 1
Changes

Today my mom left. I don't mean she left the house to go to the store. She left. She left our family. She left my Dad, she left my brothers, she left the house, she left Bilbo (our dog). She left me. She's left before, but that was usually spontaneous, unplanned, for an afternoon, sometimes up to a few days, but never more than three. I could count on that, never more than three days. But this time, she left forever.

Before when she left, there would be a note or something to let us know she'd be back. She never really explained why she would leave or where she would go and she usually came back in such a good mood that we just wouldn't even question her. It's just been part of our lives, I never even thought it was odd, until my friends told me their mothers "never do that", but even then, we just knew it was our "normal". Now that I think on it, we were so used to my

Mom's eccentricities and we adapted so well, that on the surface, we seemed like the average American family. Only my closest friends, Sophia, Eva, and Summer (a.k.a. Sophie, Evi, and Summi) know that my Mom is not a typical mom.

Up to now, my biggest worry had been starting high school. My Dad wanted to send me to Parker Prep School, some uppity private school that helps get you in to the "best" universities in the country, but Mom helped me convince him that it was best for me to stay with my friends and go to Mar Vista High and play sports and walk to school. I'm a good student, so Dad agreed, as long as I keep my grades up and focus on getting in to a good school. Whatever, as long as I get to stay, I'll do it! I successfully navigated my freshmen year and was well into my sophomore year, I was comfortable.

Last night, I heard my parents fighting. Oddly enough, they don't fight, and if they do, I never hear them. Anyway, the boys were asleep, but I heard things I'd never heard before, though I couldn't quite hear everything, only bits and pieces.

They kept talking about my Mom's "meds", which I know is her medication, though I've never known what it's for, just that she takes pills, but most people do I guess. From what I could hear, she tried meds on and off for years, but she's quitting them "for good this time", she said. And even though it seems they are fighting (my Mom sounds aggressive) my Dad isn't saying much, and if he is, it's in a low voice, which is very much my Dad.

My Dad is a lawyer. He's a pretty big deal as far as San Diego lawyers go. He basically never sleeps or relaxes. I think I've only seen him relax on family vacations and even then, he's usually super active: swimming, golfing, surfing, etc. He works all the time and when he's not working, he's surfing with the boys. He wakes us before he goes to work each morning and he relies on me to get up and make sure we all get to school on time. Depending on how my Mom is doing, sometimes she has breakfast ready and she gets the boys ready, sometimes I have to do it because she's asleep or not home. Dad is rarely home before seven o'clock each night, usually though he's home by nine. He works A LOT, but he's a great Dad and I know he wishes he had more time for us and for surfing. I know he's a tough lawyer and doesn't take any crap from anyone, I often hear people say that "he doesn't suffer fools", but with us, he's pretty soft spoken, doesn't talk very much, and has a very comforting presence, which makes you feel like everything is calm and nothing can hurt you. But I guess not even my Dad can fix my Mom.

Mom cried and cried, when she wasn't yelling at my Dad. She kept saying things like "they stifle me" and "I feel like I'm in a prison". I couldn't tell who "they" are, I guess it's us, her kids. Why did she have kids then? It was hard to understand with all the crying and yelling and sniffling and such.

Then I heard my Dad say, firmly, strongly, but not unkindly, "Charlotte, this discussion is over, you have a choice to make, only you can make it." Then I just heard footsteps and the bedroom door closing. My Mom continued to cry, but it was so sad and pitiful, more like a child's whimper after it's been crying for a long time and is just too tired to cry anymore. In the morning, she was gone.

My Dad woke me up as usual, my reliable alarm clock, a little shoulder shake and a "Good mornin' Sweets". But when I looked at him and gave him my usual nod, I saw a sad look in his eyes. He hadn't slept, I could tell, he looked tired and older somehow, it made me instantly uneasy and sad, something had changed. The routine was like every other school day routine but the look in my Dad's eyes said that nothing would ever be the same again.

I got the boys ready for school and Iris, the babysitter, came by and took them to school. I heard the door open and knew it was Summer, here to walk with me to school. She didn't notice anything different, why would she, she'd been my friend so long that she knew what our home was like, it was normal to her too. In fact, the fab four, our parents called us, had been friends since we were in preschool. We walked by Sophie and Eva's houses on the way and we walked by the beach to check the surf (a daily ritual) and decided to stop for a smoothie on the way to school. It was a basic normal day filled with Algebra and English, gross cafeteria lunches and volleyball practice after school. Sophie, Eva, and I are all athletes, we play volleyball and basketball and we surf. Summer tags along and is our biggest cheerleader, she wanted to be a cheerleader at one point but lost interest I guess. Summer's "sport" of choice is boys, she is a master flirt and always has her eye out for cute boys, especially new and interesting ones, but we are still a tight crew, spending as much time together as possible.

After practice I walked home, "Summi, wanna stay for dinner? Iris is probably here so there should be something good". She declined saying she wanted to use her mom's new nail polish before she got home and said she'd text later. I walked in and Dad was home early, which was strange and instantly gave me a feeling of foreboding. Something was not right, my Dad looked strange, I guess he looked determined, and determined he was. Determined to ruin my life!

Chapter 2
Expect the Unexpected

Expect the unexpected. My Dad and I had this secret saying, just between the two of us. I know that it's a common saying, but it really applied in our house, especially when it came to my Mother. Whenever something crazy happened, like the time my Mom decided she wanted to make the best pecan pie ever made and had us peeling pecans for days while she baked pie after pie, after pie, trying to get it just right. We ate pecan pie for breakfast, lunch and dinner! Every neighbor, teacher, doctor, firefighter and lifeguard in town had eaten "Charlotte's pecan pie". My Mom never did anything in moderation.

This time, the unexpected came from my Dad, which was so out of character for him that it really messed with my mind.

My Dad was the rock; my Mom was the wind. He was strong and stable and sturdy and she was like the wind, powerful enough to get caught up in and blowing in many different directions. So, when he said he needed to have a talk, I was not prepared for what he said, in fact I was shocked, left speechless.

"Sweets, I need to talk to you about something". I could tell whatever he had to say was hard for him, but he had that determined look and I knew that despite this being hard to tell me, he was going to do it. And suddenly I was scared, very scared and I started to feel panic, at least I think that's what it was, I'd never felt anything quite like it.
"Is she dead"?
"What? Who?" Then he realized, I thought my Mom was dead, and he stood up and hugged me, "No, no, no, she's not, don't worry, everything is going to be okay". He hugged me tighter and with a final squeeze he let out a long, deep breath, "life is going to change for us, but everything will be okay".

I wiped my tears away, I hadn't realized I was crying. I straightened myself up and nodded, letting my Dad know he could continue, that I was ready to hear whatever it was.

"Your Mom is gone and we are moving, leaving the country."

Stunned, in disbelief, I responded with something ridiculous, "But we can't move, Mom won't know where to find us when she comes back". Then I just sat in stunned silence while he explained and I felt like my life was over and I just wanted to crawl up into a ball and cry.

"Your Mom and I are getting a divorce. A long time ago when we decided to get married we made promises to each other and she broke her promises. I've tried to work it out, I've tried to help her and accommodate her and live in her world but it just doesn't work for me and it doesn't work for you or your brothers either. She had a choice to make and she chose to leave the family. She won't be coming back. I don't know if you will ever hear from her again. I just don't know. I know it's hard, I know what it's like to lose your mother, but I'm going to ask you to do some difficult things and you need to know, that I'm doing this for us, and that things will be good eventually. Okay, so, your Mom left the family, we will deal with that, but I've been dreaming about this for a long time and I feel like the time to make the move is now.

"MOVE, what do you mean MOVE? We don't need a new house, this one is close to school and my friends and the beach and the boys' school and Iris and what about Bilbo? He'll be lost at a new house, he already knows this neighborhood and…". My Dad put a hand up to stop my rambling.

"We are moving out of the country, not the neighborhood. My whole life I have wanted to live in Mexico, it's where I was born, where my family is and I've always wanted to work in environmental law, making a difference, protecting the planet. There is an opportunity to work with some talented people, working to create nature reserves on the Baja peninsula, and I'm tired Sweets, tired of the long hours, tired of the meaningless corporate law that I practice, the situation with your mom, always being worried. I think it will be a welcome change for all of us, an adventure, new places to see, new people to meet, and making a difference in the world will energize us all. I'm sure you have a million questions, but I'm just so tired Lily, please, just go with it, I promise that you'll adjust and be happy. Pretend you are going on a very long vacation". He sighed and I felt sorry for him. My rock was suddenly not a rock, but something else, fragile, sad, tired, and a little lost.

"Well can I ask just three questions now please?", I tried to say as delicately as possible.

He looked at me, a bit more playfully, with half a grin and a slightly trepidatious look, "Okay", he said with an almost cringe.

"Where are we going? When are we going? Can I skip school tomorrow and go surfing, the waves are going to be epic?".

"San Jose del Cabo, down at the tip of the Baja peninsula. Soon, but I don't have an official date.", then he chuckled, "I don't think so, you should go to school, be with your friends, go to practice."

"There's no practice tomorrow and I just need to clear my head Dad, come on, please?".

Just a nod. But that was enough. I sent a text to Summi and she came over, then we went to Eva and Sophie's and convinced them to skip tomorrow too.

We met at my house in the morning, Dad and the boys were gone, so we were able to load up on snacks. Then we all went over to Summi's and begged her brother to give us a ride to the cliffs. His truck easily fit all our surfboards and us. I think he saw the desperation in my face and agreed to drop us off. Ryan was not always on our side and seemed to be annoyed by us, but every once in a while, he could be really cool.

On the ride to the cliffs I started to digest everything my Dad had said. I had so many questions, about my Mom, about Cabo, about my life and I began to feel so overwhelmed. Too many thoughts racing through my head. I started to feel like I couldn't breathe and my heart was pounding. Sophie noticed and grabbed my hands.

"Are you okay?" she whispered, "Your hands are all clammy and you look pale. Just take deep breaths, control your breathing, count on the inhale and count the same on the exhale."

Eva looked over with a worried expression, but didn't say anything. She was more of a quiet type, like me, while Sophie and Summer were more outgoing and talkative. She waited for me to give her a thumbs up before she went back to staring out the window.

Sophie whispered again, "Better?" I nodded and pretended I was better, I could breathe again, but my mind was still racing. Summer turned up the radio when a song she liked came on and started singing, it actually made me feel better and I soon found the car ride was over and we were hiking down the cliffs with our boards and gear. I knew at least the water would make me feel at ease and I wouldn't have to think for a while. My Dad always says that it's our "zen". The ocean is a special place for our family. We are all very skilled and confident in the water, whether it's swimming, kayaking, surfing, etc., we love it and Dad says he could never live landlocked.

We put our wetsuits on, something I've never enjoyed. I feel so restricted, like I'm a sausage stuffed in a casing, but in San Diego, except for summertime, you need a wetsuit. We discussed the waves and where we would head in as we stretched. Summer made camp, set up the mini speaker and pulled out her tablet. Summer only swims when she can wear a bikini, at least that's what she says, but even though she doesn't surf, she never complains and she always comes along and does her own thing while we're in the water. And she watches our stuff, which is so convenient. Though one time she left our stuff unattended while she went off to share a pizza with some cute guy and our shoes were stolen. We laughed about it while we walked home barefoot and now we always say "watch our shoes" when we head into the water. She just waves at us and pretends to be annoyed by the comment, but she would never let it happen again, as a matter of pride.

Chapter 3
Denial

The water was cold, but so beautiful. Glassy and dark, with a green tinge to it. The waves were in fact, epic, and we had each caught a few and were laying on our boards and resting a bit, waiting for the next set. Sophie asked if I wanted to talk about what was going on with me, but I shook my head and just said "not now". I tried to clear my mind of everything. I tried not to think about my Mom abandoning me and my Dad uprooting us and moving us to another country. I focused on feeling the water underneath me, lapping at my board while I stared up at the sky, closing my eyes.

Sophie suddenly squealed with delight, ruining our surf cred, "Check out the sets rolling in", and with that she was gone, paddling hard to catch the first wave of the set, with ease and precision. Sophie really is the best instinctual surfer in the group and Eva is probably the most deliberate and technically sound. I just surfed, not thinking. I wouldn't win any contests, but I can catch just about anything and make something of it. There were maybe two or three other surfers out, guys, we didn't know them so we just stayed out of their way, there were plenty of waves for everyone that day. It was so fun, we stayed in until we could barely paddle anymore. Eva finally gave in and said, "I'm hungry, I'm heading in. Should I call my Dad and ask him to pick us up in an hour? That'll give us time to dry off and hike back up, and you can still catch a few more waves. I'll tell him to pick up some food." Sophie and I agreed and paddled back out.

As we sat up on our boards waiting for our waves, I pointed out to our left and said, "Dolphins coming". Sophie squinted in that direction and shook her head. She didn't see them yet, but I knew they were there, and she knew if I said it, then they were definitely there. Sophie caught the next wave and rode it all the way in to shore and she sat on the sand with Eva and watched me. I could feel the dolphins getting closer and then saw them playing and jumping. Eva and Sophie stood up and were watching them play, pointing and laughing as they watched. I saw the next wave setting up and knew it was going to be a good one. I would have to paddle hard to catch it, but it would be a good, long ride. I paddled hard, kept my arms shallow and fast and suddenly I was in it, and standing up, I felt solid and bent down to run my hand through the wave, a glorious feeling, I had this feeling of pure joy, but not just on the inside, I felt it all around me, almost like I was absorbing it from somewhere else. I could see from the side that Eva, Sophie and Summer were jumping and cheering and with that I noticed that I had company. Dolphins! Surfing on the wave with me! So beautiful! I couldn't believe it, it was so exhilarating and wonderful, I never wanted it to end.

Suddenly, I felt a bump on my board and I fought to maintain my balance but I couldn't and I fell off. On the way, I hit my head on the board, hard and everything went black. I could feel the water swirling around me, I could hear, well not exactly hear, but it felt like voices, I can't explain it.

"He didn't mean to do it, he was just curious, he doesn't know about boards (though the word wasn't boards, but I knew that's what they were "talking" about), help her, push her up so she can breathe, eyes up to the sky, that's how they breathe, push her toward the shore, they are coming for her, bite the cord, here they come, but keep her up, they are slow". It felt like this crazy stream of consciousness that I could somewhat understand.

Then I was on the beach, coughing up water, with the girls yelling and hitting me on the back, asking if I was okay. They were bombarding me with questions.

"Are you okay?"
"Your head is bleeding, but it's small and seems to be stopping, does it hurt?"
"Are you hurt anywhere else?"
"Talk to us."
"Lily, say something!!!"
"Don't worry, we got your board, but the leash is torn."
"What happened?".
"Lily, Lily, Lily".

I blinked and saw them hovering and prodding and checking my suit. "Why did he bump my board?", I asked.

"Who?", Sophie asked and looked around. "No one else was in the water".

Summer started to say, "The dolphins, they, they, they pushed you up and I think they saved you", she stuttered.

I looked at her. She knew we weren't supposed to ever talk about it. She couldn't make eye contact at first, she looked freaked out. She then made eye contact and slowly nodded, understanding what I was saying. NEVER speak of this, NEVER.

Sophie and Eva looked at each other and were very quiet. Sophie said, "Just tell us if you are okay".

"I'm fine. I don't want to talk about this, ever. Please, don't say anything to my Dad, or anyone. If I don't feel well, I'll make something up and go to the hospital, but really, I'm fine.

I wasn't exactly fine. We took our wet suits off, dried and changed. We packed up, though Summi had packed up most of the stuff already and we got ready to hike back up. Without a word, Sophie took my board for me and I stuffed my wetsuit in my backpack and headed up after them. Eva waited and went up behind me, probably in case I fell over or something. Quiet and strong that one, she's a comforting presence in any situation.

Eva's Dad picked us up and we ate in the car while he chatted about his day and talked soccer to Eva. She was on the club team he coaches and she's this reluctant super star who could make the national team someday. It was nice to hear about someone else's life and not have to answer any questions. The ride home was almost the exact cure I needed after the "incident".

When I got home, all my problems were there waiting for me, though if you just looked on the surface, everything seemed the same. The boys were playing video games while Iris washed dishes. She yelled to me from the kitchen "lasagna is in the oven", as I made a beeline for my room.

What happened today? Do I want to even think about it? Who or what bumped my board? Who or what saved me? Who was talking? Did I make all that up in my head while I was unconscious? Was I unconscious? I decided I wouldn't think about it now, and I put it away in a little box in the far corner of my mind and drifted off to sleep.

I woke up when my Dad got home and I heard him tell Luca to come and get me while he and Ollie set the table.

Luca knocked on the door and came in, not waiting for my approval. He jumped on my bed and sung, "Dinner time" at the top of his lungs. I had to laugh.

At dinner, my Dad tried to make small talk and then he wanted to talk about surfing. I didn't want him to know about what happened and I really didn't feel like talking in general, but he kept going on and on about surfing and it was making me a little crazy.

"I'm not going to surf anymore" I declared, out of nowhere. My Dad just sat there, rather stunned and I saw he was going to start asking me questions so I just started to ramble before he could. "I want to be a photographer. Sophie and Eva are so good; I want to film them. I'll still get to spend plenty of time in the water, but I want a different perspective. It's going to be my new thing. I'm going to take wildlife photographs and film surfing and the ocean and anything like that. I'll need a GoPro camera with the water-resistant casing and some new fins. Don't skimp, I'll need the good ones, both camera and fins and maybe a new mask too, but I'm not sure I can do it with a mask, but get me one anyway, a good one, that won't fog up, and I'll let you know if I need any more gear. I need this Dad. Please."

I got up from the table, put my dishes in the sink, washed them and left them to dry while my brothers and Dad sat there speechless. I had successfully avoided any questions. I felt such relief. I went to bed and right to sleep. Exhausted.

The next day was Saturday and when I got up everyone was gone. There was a note saying Dad had left money for lunch on the counter and that there was also leftover lasagna and that he and the boys would be back by dinner time.

My Mom would always forget she could text us and would always leave notes. I think my Dad left a note on purpose, to make me feel like nothing has changed, but everything has, no matter what he does, it will never be the same.

I texted the girls to come over and we hung out all day and watched movies. They looked me over to see if I was okay, but didn't say a word about the "incident". We talked about school and the new kid Blake, who according to Summer, was "totally into her", and our upcoming Volleyball game that we had to win in order to make the playoffs. It was so normal and comforting. What was I going to do without my best friends? I tried not to think about it.

In the middle of *Harry Potter and the Order of the Phoenix*, my Dad got home. I was instantly annoyed. Even though we'd seen all the Harry Potter movies a hundred times, I felt irritated at the intrusion and the assault on our perfectly normal day. He and the boys seemed so happy and like they'd had a great day, they were talking about the waves they'd caught and the ice cream cone Ollie had dropped on some poor lady's lap. With a quick hello to the girls, my Dad dropped a big bag on the couch next to me and went to the kitchen, still laughing with the boys.

Luca was making dramatic splattering sounds and mimicking what must have been the lady's angry face and they seemed oblivious to the fact that their mother had abandoned them and they were moving away, soon…

In the bag was a super camera, with waterproof casing, fins, and a mask, all of the highest quality, really professional equipment. I was stunned. I couldn't believe it. For a second I felt bad, I just said all of that crap because I had almost died in a surfing accident and, something strange I didn't want to face had happened, and I was trying desperately to avoid any questions or hear about my Mom or the move.

I guess I'm going to become a photographer. In truth, it would give me a great excuse not to surf. I'm pretty sure I'm too scared to get back up on a board anytime soon and the idea of still being in the water, with a purpose, was kind of exciting. I explained to the girls why my Dad had bought me this stuff and they seemed pretty excited and as always, super supportive.

I went to put my new equipment in my room and decided to put it all in my pack. I took my wetsuit and torn leash out to make room for my new stuff. I grabbed the leash to throw it away and noticed something strange. It wasn't a clean cut. It didn't just snap off as they sometimes do. Where it was cut was closer to the end that my foot attaches to, and as I looked at it closely, I noticed, something, it looked gnawed. Were those teeth marks?

Chapter 4
Mom

As the months passed and we adjusted to a life without our Mom, I helped get the boys to school every morning and went to classes and practices and spent time filming my friends surfing. My Dad didn't talk much, he was extra generous and gave me permission to do just about anything I asked. I knew he was feeling guilty about the move, but I overheard his phone conversations and watched him search for homes in Mexico which indicated that he was moving forward with his crazy plan.

Iris was coming in early a couple days a week to help with breakfast and the boys. This morning as I packed up my things to leave for school I heard my dad talking to her about packing. I left in a rush, I didn't want to hear anymore. I didn't want to face what was coming and my Dad must have sensed it because he wasn't talking much. He waved goodbye as I ran out the door and he looked sad. Maybe he would feel sorry for us and change his mind or maybe his mind was made up and he was sad that I wasn't enthusiastic about his plan.

When I got home from school no one was home. Iris had texted me that the boys were staying at their buddy Davis' house and that I should walk over and pick them up at 5. I went to my room to change and chill after a mediocre school day and I noticed my Dad's bedroom door was open and there were boxes labeled and stacked in a corner. I went in to see what he had packed, which might give me a clue to when we are leaving but when I opened a box I felt like I'd been slapped across the face. It was all my Mom's stuff. Nothing of hers was left in the room or the closet. I ran out to the garage where she had her workspace and it was all packed up as well.

I went back to my Dad's room and started moving all the boxes from there into the garage with the others. It occurred to me that my Dad looked sad this morning because he asked Iris to pack up HER things, not his. With my world being turned upside down, I never once stopped to think about how my Dad might be feeling. That he might also feel abandoned was a jarring thought. It made me so uncomfortable and so, so sad.

Just then my Dad called to ask if I'd picked up the boys. I'd forgotten! He snapped at me on the phone, saying that I was distracted and irresponsible, and then said he'd pick them up on his way home and hung up. He hung up on me! I felt so offended. Why are the boys always my responsibility anyway? I've been helping out with them since they were born, mainly because my Mother couldn't handle it on her own, though I'm not sure she realized it half the time. I think I did it so that the rest of the world wouldn't see that she wasn't always stable. But I felt angry that now it had become expected that I would take care of the two little monsters (they were actually funny, cute little boys with bright, shining, unique personalities) and that I was responsible for their care and wellbeing. I'm their sister, not their mother! What do I know about raising kids? I'm 15 years old, just a sophomore in high school!

To think that I was trying to do a nice thing for my Dad and he gets mad at me! I decided not to be home when he and the boys got home and I left, just down the street to Summi's. I knew that Eva was at something for soccer and that Sophie was hanging out with Chris, her possible new boyfriend. Summer's house was only a block away and I just needed to be out of the house and away from my Dad.

Summi was in her room giving herself a pedicure with her head phones on, singing along to whatever she was listening to, I couldn't tell. She saw me, smiled, and waved me in, handing me the nail polish as she took off her headphones.
"What's up? You look like you're in a bad mood, try this neon pink on your fingernails, it'll cheer you up!"

I nodded and took the nail polish. I rarely painted my nails, I liked them short and clean, it was easier especially for sports. I told her my Dad snapped at me about forgetting the boys and she rolled her eyes.

"I'm so glad I only have one older brother, I don't think I'd be a very good babysitter, little kids are so needy and they smell." She scrunched up her nose and laughed. I laughed too and suddenly felt less angry. Summer could have that effect on people, she was quick with a joke and had an uncanny ability to diffuse uncomfortable situations. There was never an awkward silence when she was around.

"I don't want to move." I told her, it came out as almost a whisper.

"Listen, it sucks, we don't want you to go, but it's not going to change our friendship. I looked up plane tickets and they aren't that expensive and it's a two-hour flight, shorter than Harry Potter and the Sorcerer's Stone!".

I looked up at her, feeling the tears in my eyes, but couldn't help laugh when I saw her face. It was so sweet and matter of fact. I knew she meant it. What was I going to do without my pod?

Summer started to talk about how she ran into Drew, her ex-boyfriend and how she was sure he was jealous because she was talking to the new guy Blake. And I soon forgot my problems and focused on hers. It was a relief. We did some homework together, which is nice because Summer is so smart and school work has always come easily to her, I do fine at school and really only math is hard for me, but she is super, super smart.

I walked home and my Dad was giving the boys a bath when I arrived and he told me there was pizza for dinner, as though nothing had happened earlier. I decided to let it go too and went to my room with a slice to finish up my Algebra.

Volleyball season ended and I decided not to play any more sports at school. Sophie and I decided to both join Eva's club soccer team, even if we had to ride the bench, at least we could all be together and since Eva's Dad is one of the coaches, we made the team. Actually, we weren't terrible. Even though Eva was the star of the team, we actually got some good playing time and had fun together and Summi was never far away, cheering us on.

My Dad hadn't mentioned the move in a while and I was secretly hoping he had changed his mind, but no such luck.

"Dad I'm home", it was Saturday and we'd had an early game. The house was quiet and Dad had left a note: The boys and I went for a surf and then to look at a trailer in La Mesa, be back by dinner time.

A trailer? What was he talking about? I called him to check in and figure out what he was talking about. He said he needed to buy a trailer so he could start packing things we wanted to take with us when we move. I quickly ended the conversation, I didn't want to hear about it. I texted the girls but they were all busy so I made myself a grilled cheese and watched some TV.

I was looking in the couch for the remote when I found something else instead. It was a little clay turtle. It was my Mom's, she made it, in fact she made three, one for each of us. The boys must have been playing with it. It made me feel, I don't know exactly, angry? I took it to the garage to put in the boxes of my Mom's things.

I pulled down one of the boxes at the top and opened it. I grabbed some newspaper and wrapped up the little turtle. That was one of my Mom's obsessions, pottery or ceramics I guess. She would take up "projects" that would turn into obsessions. The ceramics obsession began with a school project I had to do. I think I had to build a model of an adobe house or something, I don't even remember, but what I do remember is how my Mom got so excited about the project. We went to buy the supplies and she bought more stuff than I needed and a large amount of clay, we laughed about how we could build an actual house with all that clay.

My project took about a week to complete, but her obsession with clay was for about three months. Most of her projects or hobbies or whatever you want to call them lasted about three to five months and some would reappear on occasion. It was so great to be around her when she was working on these projects, at least at the beginning. She was so happy and her energy was beyond measure and it could be infectious, but again, at the beginning. You could see a change after a week or two. You could see a change in her eyes, she would spend all her time creating things in her workshop. She had a workspace in the garage, because this was not her first obsession and wouldn't be the last. She would spend all day on it and work through the night, often not sleeping or just falling asleep in her clothes on the couch for a few hours, if at all. She wouldn't get up to help us with breakfast or get ready for school. Sometimes she was still awake having worked through the night and she might join us for a piece of toast and then "get back to work" because she just had so much to do. She would make us little clay animals, vases, mugs, and she just had to finish the set of plates that we needed and the set she was making for the new neighbors. My Mom is definitely artistic, crafty, and handy with tools, but it was usually on her terms, her vision, her way.

Another obsession she had was building and restoring bikes. It started when the twins asked for bikes. The twins are athletic prodigies, at least I think so. They could rollerblade at the age of two, they didn't even make skates their size, but they zoomed around the neighborhood. They were great on their skateboards too, riding them almost at the same time they could walk. When they wanted bikes, my parents bought them bikes with training wheels, but the twins hated them. They wanted bigger bikes with no "extra wheels" as they described. So, they took back the little bikes and bought them bigger bikes, like a 10-12-year-old might ride. They could ride them but they needed a ledge to be able to jump on and off because they couldn't reach the ground, so my Mom decided to go ahead and modify them herself, and that's when the bike obsession started. She made us all bikes, making us try them out, changing the seats, raising and lowering handlebars, adding glow in the dark lights along the frames, changing the baskets, etc. My Dad had to make her stop when we had about twelve bikes in the garage. That obsession came back when I asked her to help me change a flat on my tire. She proceeded to change the entire bike again and now one of the pedals keeps falling off and she changed the whole thing again. All I wanted was to fix my flat and it went on for weeks again, I felt so bad, like it was my fault and now I won't even ride my bike, it's just rusting away in the garage.

One obsession we loved was when she was making cakes. She would experiment with different mixes and frostings and we ate cake for breakfast, lunch and dinner. She then started to experiment with her own recipes (no more box mixes) and those were not so good. I've heard that baking is like chemistry and you must be very precise, something my Mom was not and those cakes often failed to make the cut and she would either eat them or throw them out. We were happy when the obsessions would end, but what came next wasn't so pleasant either.

After an obsession, or a long few months of non-stop activity, came the dark days. That's what we would call them, her dark days. She would sleep for days not leaving her room. Sometimes she would wake up take a shower and go back to her bed. Other times she might just be sitting in her armchair crying. If we asked her why she was crying, she usually "didn't know" or it was something nonsensical. We knew that when it was a dark day that we should take her food, let her sleep, and just hug her and comfort her if she cried. The dark days didn't usually last too long, never more than a couple of weeks and as little as a couple of days when we were lucky.

It's amazing how so many memories could come flooding back with a little clay turtle. As I put it away in the box, I noticed it was a box of her toiletries. Maybe she had some good make-up in there that I could keep. I started to look through the box and I found the usual stuff, perfume, some make up, vitamins, etc., but then I found a couple of prescription pill bottles. What were they? I tucked them into my pocket so I could look them up on my computer later. Why didn't I know what type of medication she took? The bottles seemed full, I guess she didn't always take them.

When I looked at the bottles, I didn't recognize any of the names, though why would I? One of them was Lithium and the other was Lamictal. When I looked them up, schizophrenia popped up. Also, anti-psychotic and Lamictal seemed to be tied to depression. I didn't read too much about the medications, well, because when I saw the word schizophrenia, I immediately started looking that up and I didn't like what I read. It scared me and it's quite a blow to know that your mother is crazy. I mean I always knew she wasn't the typical Mom and she certainly wasn't like anyone else I knew, but she's my Mom and I know that everyone is different. I just thought I had a quirky, eccentric Mom, but crazy? I read a little about it but I was frightened and it brought up so many questions. I read that there is a genetic connection, it can be hereditary and that it doesn't appear until early adulthood usually. So, it was possible that I had it too? That maybe right now it was starting to affect me? Maybe the "voices" I was hearing during the "incident" were just in my head, maybe it was just me.

I kept recalling all of her obsessions and wondered if she heard voices. Maybe the voices pushed her to do things. There were so many happy times too though. I remember her waking us up at four in the morning to go to Disneyland, just because, and staying there for three days, not worrying about school or activities. I remember when she dug up our whole back yard and built/planted a vegetable garden that only lasted one season. She would take things apart and then try to put them back together, sometimes successfully, sometimes not. One summer we had smoothies every day for four months, every fruit you can imagine, but she would usually settle on her favorite and we'd have that over and over and over again. Once, when we went to Big Sur, she loaded up the truck with drift wood and did woodworking for weeks. She would flip her clock and be up all night and sleep all day. She was always late for things, getting distracted by projects or other small details that no one would notice (like re-wrapping a gift twelve times to get it just right) and she would do things for us that we didn't ever ask for like getting me a new backpack, a month after purchasing me my last one and painting my room without asking if I wanted it changed. She was kind and so friendly, she knew everyone in the neighborhood and she was generous to a fault sometimes. But there was darkness too. She once put up surveillance cameras all around the house, outside and inside because she was sure someone was trying to steal Bilbo our dog.

I can't believe this is happening. My mother is crazy, why didn't I ever put all this together? I might be crazy too and I'm moving and leaving everything and everyone I've ever known. This was not an ideal situation to say the least. I decided to steal *Scarlett O'Hara's* strategy. "I won't think about it today; I'll think about it tomorrow…"

Chapter 5
Bad Decision Farewells

My Dad told us that we would leave after school ended. He told the boys and I that we needed to help Iris pack our things. He said that if we didn't help her that she would pack for us and would make decisions about what to keep. I told him I would pack my own things, but he said I'd need help. I was told to keep only one box of any winter clothing because it's basically hot year-round where we are going. He said we should pack a suitcase for what we would be wearing for the road trip and the rest of our time here.

I went through my things carefully, trying to get rid of as much as possible. I kept most of my shorts, t-shirts, sundresses and bathing suits. I also kept a couple pairs of jeans and my two favorite hoodies. I tend to get attached to my things, but I really tried to let go and anything that reminded me of my mom went straight to the "donate" box.

I tried to be as positive as I could, thinking about a new life, an adventure and a totally new beginning where I could reinvent myself if I chose, but I cried the entire time.

I made a list of things I needed and things I wanted. My Dad let me go shopping for more clothes because according to him, the shopping down there isn't great. So, I bought multiple new bathing suits, some rash guards and some shorts. I already had a new mask and fins, but I really wanted a new kayak, so I printed a picture of the one I wanted and left it on the fridge for my Dad to see, I hope he gets the hint.

The girls went shopping with me and made me laugh. They were super excited that they would be coming to visit and they had already booked a trip for Labor Day weekend. My Dad said I'd be able to keep my same phone and number and that I'd be able to text and call my friends like I usually do. All of this did make me feel better, but the second the girls weren't with me, I'd start to think again and it was hard.

Finally, I went through my wetsuits. My Dad said the water is warm and that I wouldn't need any wetsuits, but I couldn't get rid of them. I stashed my 4/3 winter suit at Sophie's and my 3/2 at Eva's and just kept my spring suit to take with me. I also left my two surfboards with Evi, for her or Sophie to use if they want, thinking that maybe I'd surf again, maybe someday.

I didn't tell the girls about what I discovered about my Mom, I just wasn't ready. I was worried that they would jump to the same conclusion I did, that I also might be crazy, and I just wasn't ready for them to look at me differently. I needed something in my life to stay the same.

...

Life proceeded as usual. The girlies and I continued our beach going, with Summer setting up camp, Sophie and Evi surfing, with me adjusting to my new role as photographer and videographer. I had gotten some cool footage of the girls today that I was rather proud of and I was learning the best places to be where I could get them up close but not be in the way of any other surfers. I'd already been chewed out by some of the older local guys for cutting them off or for them having to pull out of a wave because I was in the way. They yelled at me, but when I showed them what I was doing, they suddenly wanted me to get some video of them, so I started to make sure I knew who was out there and sent them pics and video whenever I could. Everyone said I was getting better and they were always excited to see themselves surfing.

Today was one of those days where I'd gotten a ton of cool shots of the girls and some of the guys that were out there too. I swam in and headed to our camp where Summer was sunning herself in a tiny bikini as usual. She got up to dust the sand off herself and said she was going to get something from the snack shop at the pier. I said I'd hold down the fort and begged her to bring me an iced mocha or something. She giggled, tossed her corn-silk hair and said she would, after she was done hunting.

After a while Sophie and Eva came out of the water and we hung out and ate some sandwiches that Summer had made for us. Then Summi came back, practically bouncing along the sand. "Summi, where's my mocha?". She laughed and motioned to look behind her. There were three guys, one of them holding a tray with what appeared to be our caffeinated beverages.

The guys came and sat with us. I could tell that Summer couldn't make up her mind which one she liked more (truthfully they were all pretty cute), so she made it clear to us that she hadn't decided and we should back off until she did.

We knew what she was saying, but we didn't care about those boys, so we just hung out, listened to music and let Summi flirt to her heart's content. They told us about a party this Saturday down the street from Sophie's at Andre's house that sounded fun and we said we'd see them there. Then packed up to walk home.

"Summi, what were you thinking bringing those guys over, it was kind of embarrassing," Eva said.

"Yeah, look at us, all water logged with messed up hair", Sophie added. "You look all cute in your bikini, make up and dry, styled hair".

"It's not my fault you guys prefer surfing, you know my sport is boys. Besides, you got free mochas, didn't you?"

We laughed and talked about the party and what we would wear. Summer was going to make sure that Blake was invited and asked Sophie if she wanted Chris to be there. "Don't worry Sophs, I'll make sure he's invited, he likes you, it's obvious!", she poked Sophie in the side until she agreed.

When I got home, my Dad dropped a bombshell. "We leave Sunday, early, make sure you mark your boxes and put what you need for the summer aside to go in the trailer". He looked at me with an excited and happy face and then noticed I wasn't smiling. I wasn't moving or speaking either. He grabbed my hand and pulled me outside into the driveway. "Come here Sweets, I want to show you something". He practically dragged me into the trailer to show me what he had gotten. "I sold a bunch of our old gear and got some new cool stuff. The kayak is yours and I got a few stand-up paddle boards and new surfboards for the boys. He said, "Of course, if you want to surf, you can use ours, or I can get you a new one?". I thanked him and said I was pretty excited about the kayak. There was a spot for Bilbo to sit and enough room for my gear and even a little ice chest. I hugged my Dad and ran to my room before I started crying. I didn't want to hurt him anymore, so I decided I would pretend to be excited in front of him. Fake it till you make it, right?

I spent the next few days packing and sorting and labeling and finishing what my Dad asked me to finish. I left out a suitcase of clothes for the road trip and a dress to wear to the party. Sophie was going to lend me a pair of shoes so that I wouldn't have to leave them here. I told my Dad we were all getting ready at Sophie's. He said I needed to be home by midnight, that we were leaving early the next morning to avoid the traffic and so that we could stop and surf along the way. I begged him to stay at Sophie's with the other girls, but he said he needed me home and ready to go in the morning. He had shipped our furniture (at least what we were keeping, mainly mine and the boys' bedroom furniture and some artwork), but he'd sold most of it or donated it. He really wanted to make a fresh start.

The boys were ecstatic. They never mentioned our Mom, I think my Dad keeps them busy so they won't have time to think about it. Ollie was riding his bike, trying to use the trailer ramp to jump over boxes and Luca was climbing the trailer pretending to surf on the roof. Ollie rode by my side and at the end of the block before making the turn towards Sophie's, I asked him to take Bilbo back to the house. I handed him the leash and told him to go slow and not strangle the dog. He laughed and laughed while singing some song he made up about Bilbo running faster than he's ever run before. I watched him get back to the house and as soon as he let go of the leash, Bilbo started running toward me. I held up my hand and he stopped, grumpily heading back to the house.

When I got to Soph's, Evi and Summi were already there. We blasted some new band Sophie swears she discovered and got ready for the party. Summer did all our make-up and we each did our hair long and straight to match. Sophie with her dark brown hair and huge brown eyes looked so pretty in her jean shorts and green top. I wore a green summer dress that made my eyes look even more green (at least that's what Summi said). Eva wore her dark blonde hair straight, though it was naturally wavy and really curly when short, she looked like Shirley Temple when she was little, with her ringlets bouncing down the soccer field. But tonight, she looked like a tall, bronzed sculpture. Summer looked her usual stunning self, with her soft blond hair and blue eyes sparkling. I knew she was up to something when I saw that sparkle in her eye.

"Ok girls" Sophie announced. "I've been thinking, instead of moping about because one of our crew is leaving, we are going to have a crazy, fun blow out and send off our lovely Lily on a grand adventure. We are not going to be sad, because we have cell phones and we can talk all the time. We are going to pretend that she's going on a vacation and that we will meet her there later in the fall. Things are not going to be the same, but they don't have to be awful either. We will find ways to be together, always".

With that, Eva spoke up and said, "Well that was quite a speech, too bad we don't have anything to drink".

"Oh yes we do" Summi dug into her bad and pulled out four bottles of Gatorade. We laughed and laughed, at least until we opened them and took a drink.

Eva almost choked, "What on earth is this?", she swallowed as best she could and smelled the contents along with Sophie and I.

"Oh there's a little vodka in there, did I forget to mention that?", she smiled wickedly.

We got to the party with a little bit of a buzz, or maybe more than a little. There were definitely some kids we knew from school but it seemed most of the guys were surfers from around the county and some kids from Coronado too.

Summer and Sophie led the way to the bar, insisting we at least grab a drink. "I suppose it's fine, we can just drink it slowly, keep the same one all night, no one will know", I whispered to Eva. She nodded. There was a big thermos, like the ones used for athletic events and some ice and cups next to it. We served ourselves some rum punch, or whatever it was, mine was mostly ice. I took a sip and looked around. It was actually very sweet and before I knew it, it was gone and

I was refilling. That's pretty much how it went for me that night. Without realizing I just kept on drinking the sweet, delicious, beverage. We danced and laughed. We discussed who was cute and what people were wearing. Summer was on the lookout, even as she talked to the boys from the beach, then Blake and Chris walked into the party. I watched Summer see him and instead of going to greet him as I probably would have, I saw her kick it up a notch with the boys from the beach. She laughed, tossed her hair and squeezed one guys arm. She was putting on a show for Blake and it worked, he made a beeline towards her and made himself part of the group before somehow taking her away from the group to be on their own. Sophie was happily chatting with Chris. He had his arm around her shoulders while one of Chris' surf buddies told them some story about "getting barreled" and narrowly missing the reef.

Eva and I hung back and soon enough we were dancing and mingling with the rest. At one point, we went for a refill and Eva started to get chatty, not something she really does sober. She talked about soccer and about how she was going to try out for the under 17 national team and though she felt a lot of pressure to do well, she was also very excited. She also started talking about the new assistant coach. She actually admitted to me that she has a crush on him!

"I don't know what it is about him" she said, then she giggled, "he's hot".

I laughed, "So what's the problem, have you told him you like him or tried any of Summi's flirting techniques?". Summer was always coaching us on how to flirt, we always found it funny and amusing and secretly hoped it would be of use someday.

"He's in college" she whispered, rather loudly.

"So what?"

"Well I don't think my Dad would be too happy about it".

"I doubt he'd even noticed and he doesn't seem the type that would be super overprotective about a boy, he trusts you".

"Yeah, that's true, but I think he'd worry that it would be a distraction".

"Well, feel it out, see what happens, and for now, well, maybe we should practice".

"Practice"?

"Well, I've never really kissed a guy, and when I meet the guy that gives me the butterflies, I don't want to be a total loser". She laughed and laughed and I started to get mad, not realizing that I was already pretty tipsy. She hugged me, "Let's do it".

So, we started to look around for boys to kiss. We decided to target Summi's rejected beach boys. We started talking to them and they offered us a shot of something disgusting, but we drank it, hoping it would increase our chances for the kissing practice. One of them, Joe, seemed interested in me, he kept reaching for my hand and rubbing my back. It was kind of weird and very fuzzy, but I was determined. Eva looked at me and I knew what she was telling me, I asked Joe where the bathroom was and he walked us to it. I went in with her to make sure she was okay.

"I feel like the world is spinning".

"It is" I said and somehow we thought that was hilarious and collapsed on the bathroom floor laughing. Then suddenly Eva was sick. She hugged the toilet and waved me away, telling me, between her vomiting to just leave her and wait outside. I closed the door and waited on the stairs, where I could see the bathroom door but not be too close either.

Joe was there. He sat down next to me and asked about Evi, I mumbled something about her being fine and me waiting for her.

Just then, with no warning at all, he kissed me. He pushed his mouth into mine and stuck his tongue in my mouth, moving it around. I let him kiss me for what seemed like an hour, but was probably a few minutes, thankfully, Evi opened the door and yelled "Liiilllyyyyyy", much louder than I'd ever heard her before. I jumped up abruptly and ran to her. She pulled me in the bathroom.

"I'm done, can you make sure I don't have throw-up on me anywhere, and I really want to go home, are you ready, or do you want to keep making out with that Joe guy?", she rambled.

I wiped her face with a wet towel and straightened her up. "Let's go I said". I texted Summer and Sophie and they met us at the front door where we ghosted our way out of that party.

"OMG, you two are wasted, wait shhhhh, you're so loud", Sophie said as we interrupted her.

"Summi, I made out with Joe", I slurred. "It was disgusting. It was slobbery and he kept shoving his tongue in my mouth. It was so gross".

"It's not always gross, I promise" Summer said.

Sophie nodded her head in agreement, "Chris asked me to be his girlfriend".

"And…?", Eva asked.

"Well I said YES of course" she smiled.

We were at my door and of course it was locked. Looking back on it, I'm sure my Dad heard us from a block away, loud drunk idiots.

He opened the door rubbing his eyes. "It's almost three in the morning Lily", and he looked at the girls who were wide eyed and apologetic.

"Hi Dad, I'm pissed………that's how they say drunk in England!"

Chapter 6
Road Trip

"Lily, Lily, wake up, time to go, go take a shower and change, I'm going to put the boys in the car. Grab Bilbo when you're done and come out to the car."

It was hard to get up, I felt like I hadn't slept. Had I? I was in my sleeping bag, still in my dress, my mouth tasted foul and when I looked in the mirror, I was a mess. I took a cold shower, as a self-punishment, hoping I'd look a little better.

I changed into something comfortable for the road, grabbed my backpack, phone and Bilbo and headed to the car. My Dad was sitting in the driver's seat waiting. I closed the door and we pulled out of the drive way. Bilbo settled in between us. He stopped the car and got out leaving it running. He ran back inside, then came out, locked the door and we were off. Just like that, the only home I'd ever known, a spec in the rearview mirror.

Before we crossed the border my Dad stopped at a 24-hour fast food place. Something I'd never seen him do, but I guess nothing else was open at 5:00 am. He ordered some fries and a large coke. He handed it to me.

"Take this" he said.

"You're speaking to me?", I asked, a little afraid.

"I'm pissed and not the same kind of pissed you were last night. But, I was also a teenager once and believe it or not, I might know how you feel. Eat this and then take a nap, it might be a rough road for you today. If you're going to throw up, please let me know". His deep voice shook me to my core, I'd never heard him sound so disappointed in me, I didn't like it. And yet, despite his fury and disappointment at my stupid choices, he was still looking out for me. He could have let me suffer my fate, I deserved it.

We crossed the border and we had to get out of the car. They looked over my Dad's paperwork and they started speaking quickly. I'd forgotten how good my Dad's Spanish is and how easily it rolls off his tongue, without having to think, he can switch languages. I actually understand a lot of Spanish, when they aren't speaking too fast, but since I never speak it, I'm shy about talking but I've been told my Spanish sounds good. I guess I was taught Spanish as a child though I don't remember and according to my Dad it was my first language. I'm not sure why he stopped speaking to me in Spanish, but whenever I ask questions about that or his family or his history, my Dad always changes the subject and wraps me up in a new conversation until I've forgotten that I even asked a question. Well this is going to be at least a three-day road trip so maybe I'll try to get him to tell me something personal for once, after he's done being mad at me of course.

The first part of the trip was familiar, we'd been surfing near Tijuana, Rosarito and Ensenada before and I was hoping they'd stop somewhere to surf so I could take a nap and get myself together before the long haul.

Thankful they did. They stopped at a surf spot that we always liked, near playa Saldamando. It wasn't the typical spot, K38, but further south. You have to camp at the campground at Salsipuedes in order to have access to a little trail that you hike down to the spot. My Dad said it was only a surf stop and that we'd be leaving by lunchtime. He and the boys hiked down to surf and Bilbo and I stayed at the car. I had my pillow and I climbed to the back seat of the suburban to take a nap. When I woke up I was starting to feel a lot better, but I did have a headache. I went to the ice chest to get some cold water and sitting on top was the Advil, a little headache relief, he even thought to leave me that. I decided that I needed to be more supportive of his big ideas and new adventures. I was going to try to make the best of this.

My Dad and the boys came up the trail, looking happy and a bit tired. I helped them load the boards back in the trailer. I had let Bilbo explore a bit and called him to come back. I grabbed his water bowl and got in, and put him in the back seat with the boys.

We stopped along the way for some tacos and while the boys were running around with Bilbo I apologized to my Dad, "I'm sorry Dad, I made a bad decision, I didn't realize how much I'd had to drink".

"You shouldn't have had anything at all", he replied, still angry, "I always thought I could trust you".

"I know", I said, barely audible.

"I don't want this trip ruined".

"I know Dad, I'm not going to ruin it, you CAN trust me, I just made a mistake".

"Learn from it Sweets, and let's move on, okay?".

"Okay".

The ride was beautiful, weaving through mountains, the coast and a lot of agriculture. My Dad told me about all the tomatoes grown here and that a huge portion of Driscoll's berries were grown here. We saw buses of workers being transported and little towns where the pickers live. A lot of them wore masks over their faces so they don't breathe in the dust my Dad explained.

As my Dad was pointing something out I heard a strange sound coming from underneath the car. "Dad, do you hear that?", I asked.

"No, boys, turn down the movie please", he said as he listened. He pulled over to the side of the road and we got out.

"What is it?", I asked stupidly, as if my Dad was a mechanic that could instantly know the problem. He got down on his stomach and peered underneath the car.

"Something is dragging" he said. "Hand me an extra bungee from underneath the driver's seat".

He somehow rigged whatever it was so that it was no longer dragging, but it needed to be fixed he said.

We drove slowly to the next little town, which thankfully was not too far. We stopped at some shack, like a small house, with a bunch of junk in the yard and knocked and knocked but no one answered. We drove to the next spot that said, "Chino's" and there was a workshop next to a house. We could hear music blaring from the workshop and my Dad found Chino himself, a young guy who seemed very busy. He was in fact very busy, I heard him say, but he looked at us and the boys in the back seat and reached in the window and patted Bilbo. He looked underneath the car as my Dad had and they talked a bit. My Dad told us to stay in the car. The guy jacked up the car, with us in it, and removed a part. He went over to his welding station and repaired the part and put it back on. My Dad shook his hand and thanked him, giving him twice what he'd asked for.

"Why did you give him more than he asked for?", I asked.

"Because he really got us out of a bind and basically saved our trip and possibly our lives and only asked for about eleven dollars".

"Our lives?" I asked in shock.

"That part he fixed, that had come loose, was what holds up the gas tank, if that gas tank had fallen….", he stopped shaking his head in disbelief.

"KABOOM" Ollie yelled from the back seat. My Dad and I looked at each other and laughed. He was still watching a movie and had no idea how accurate what he just said was.

"What's so funny Daddy?", Luca asked, and we just laughed harder. We were back to normal after that. I was so glad the glacier that was between us had melted.

We stopped in a little town called El Rosario. It was very small but had a nice little hotel. We had dinner at a place called Mama Espinoza's. It was so good. Apparently, it's a famous little place because the Baja 1000 race passes through there and the drivers love it. I walked Bilbo and let him chase some chickens while I called the girls.

I was able to talk to all of them at the same time and it was kind of crazy with everyone wanting to talk at the same time. Eva and Sophie were together on speaker phone and we conferenced in Summer.

"You see, we can talk like this all the time" Summi said.

"I feel like crap, Eva said, but I think throwing up actually helped" she laughed.

"Sophie, well, Christopher is officially my boyfriend" she declared and we all made fun of her for calling him Christopher, as if we hadn't known him his whole life as Chris.

"I can't believe I kissed Joe, well he kissed me, it was so slobbery and gross".

"It's not always like that" Summi said, "some boys are really good kissers".

"It's also better if you really like the guy" Sophie chimed in.

"Well I'll wait until I do, because I'm really not excited to try that again".

We rehashed the night and everyone laughed at Eva and I. Neither one of us wanted to drink again, that was for sure. I told the girls I'd call them at our next stop tomorrow night.

As I was walking back toward the hotel I told Bilbo to follow me and told him to move nearer to me and away from the main road. He fell into step right beside me. There was an older couple walking their dogs and I told Bilbo to let them be and stay by my side. They started talking to me. They were Canadians, heading to their home in Bahia Los Angeles about five hours from here they told me.

"What a sweet dog and so obedient" the woman said, "did you train him?"

"Train him, oh no" I said, "he's just a good dog and always comes when I call him, probably because I give him treats sometimes". The couple looked at me quizzically.

"But you didn't call him, he just came and fell right into step with you and didn't even come over to check out our dogs" she said.

I hadn't called him? Hadn't she heard me?

"And my dog Maggie is very protective". I have to keep her leashed at all times, she really doesn't like anyone but me, she doesn't even let my husband touch her or even her leash!", she said, incredulously.

I looked at the Labrador she had next to her and smiled, "She seems pretty harmless" I said.

"Oh noooo, she said, this is Freddy, he's kind of dumb, and as sweet as she is mean" she shared "that's Maggie" and she pointed at me.

I hadn't noticed that I was petting a husky that was nuzzling my hand and licking my leg. Her husband just stood there dumbfounded.

"Well, I have never seen anything like that before," he said in amazement.

"Oh, haha, I ggguess she llllikes me, haha" I stuttered nervously and tried to laugh it off. I looked down at the dog who seemed to only have eyes for me. I thought to myself, go back to your owner Maggie and be a good dog. She did, immediately. She trotted back to her owner, sat down next to her and awaited her next command. I laughed to myself, yeah right. As I was saying good bye, I thought to myself again, just for a laugh. Now be nice to him, he's all right, go give him a lick and let him pet you. She did just that. I froze for a moment, not believing my eyes.

"Come on Bilbo, let's go" I made sure to say out loud, and we ran back to the hotel, our room and our beds.

Chapter 7
Road Trip continued…

Phase two of this road trip was underway. My Dad said this would be the longest day of driving and he hoped the twins could handle being in the car for at least nine hours. He said he was going to have to make it longer so we could stop at some places and let the boys and Bilbo run around.

The Baja only has one major highway and it snakes its way down, zig-zagging from Pacific coast to Gulf of California coast, crossing various mountain ranges. About an hour into the day's journey, we came upon an incredible landscape, like none I've ever seen. It was like a Dr. Seuss forest, with every size of boulder you can imagine, some stacked so precariously, it seemed like other-worldly forces must be keeping them in place. There were cacti that my Dad said can't be found anywhere else in the world. They are shaped like a carrot, but upside down, with the skinny part and the roots at the top. The strange cacti add to the unique landscape, making you feel like you're on another planet almost. It was surreal, like Dali and Dr. Seuss collaborated and this was the result. It comes to an end at a little oasis called Cataviña. We stopped for gas and something to drink and I escaped for a minute to take some pictures. In fact, I'd already made my Dad stop a few times for pictures, I would have to look up the names of the new flora and fauna (new to me anyway) when I had a chance.

We kept driving and we reached a place where on each side of us there was nothing but cactus, so dense you couldn't see through it, a cactus forest, with only the mountains in the distance. It was really amazing how by changing my attitude, I was changing this trip. I was actually having fun. I felt like an explorer on a quest, just then (he must have been noticing my reactions to everything) my Dad said, "Just wait until you see Mulege". So, I couldn't wait. We stopped at a spot in San Ignacio called Rice and Beans, it was a nice little town and the food was delicious. My Dad mentioned that it was a good place to come whale watching, during the season, but right now the whales were summering in Alaska. Before I knew it, we came upon three volcanos called El Viejo, El Azufre, and El Virgen, also known as Las Tres Virgenes, the three virgins. Around them the landscape is incredible with black volcanic rock all around and cactus, cactus, cactus. And then, after the volcanos you come to a coastal town called Santa Rosalia, an old mining town, quaint and interesting, with colorful houses and a library named after Mahatma Gandhi, and a church designed by Eiffel, but the ocean itself was nothing of interest, dark and unwelcoming. It's also a ferry town, with the ferry coming across the gulf from mainland Mexico.

Driving south from Santa Rosalia, I'm not sure exactly where, but everything changes when you get to Mulege. The water is aqua blue, clear, inviting. When I saw it, all I wanted to do was go for a swim. The boys were shouting with glee, unable to contain their excitement. My Dad was grinning ear to ear at our joy and his. It's really indescribable, something you see in a movie, so beautiful. We passed the town and stopped at a little beach called El Burro. My Dad has a friend who has a palapa there, a little house with the typical thatched palm leaf roof, but he wasn't there. He said we'd come back and stay there when he was in town and kept going, but slowly, because we were in awe of the beauty that surrounded us. He pulled up into a little cove with a beach called El Requeson. We all ran to the water, including Bilbo. It was warm and refreshing and delicious. There was a sandbar that reached out to a little island when the tide was low. Bilbo and I walked across it and explored a bit, taking photos. Then I took Bilbo back to the beach and joined the boys in the water. Ollie was on one of the stand-up paddle boards with my Dad and Luca was snorkeling next to them, I joined Luca with my mask and took some pictures of him underwater. There were tons of beautiful tropical fish and at one point a sea turtle swam by us and I got a picture of it next to my curious little brother who tried to swim after it.

When we got out of the water, Dad had packed up the paddle board and Bilbo had found some shade under the trailer, where my Dad had put some water for him. He happily jumped into the car when it was time to go, curling up for a nap in the cool air conditioned car. The rest of the drive to Loreto didn't disappoint. There were mountains, where volcanic rock had slid down the sides, but it looked like artwork, so deliberate-looking that my Dad joked that it must have taken the aliens a long time to get it right. Every bend in the road brought some wonder or another, from purple barrel cactus to herds of goats crossing the road, we were engrossed, even the boys were not watching movies, but watching out windows, nature's own movie.

We reached Loreto, hungry and tired. I helped the boys take showers and then took one myself. We walked around the center of the town, with its restaurants, plaza, and church. I was starting to see that all of the towns had this "downtown" type area. There was always a plaza and around that plaza was always a church and some sort of sense of community. It was where people gathered, ate, went for a stroll at night and there was often music and entertainment. We found a little pizza place and had dinner there. I was secretly ecstatic that there was pizza in Mexico. Being a vegetarian isn't always easy and cheese or veggie pizza was always a favorite option of mine. When my Mom was being steady (every once in a while, we'd have several months of bliss) she always made me pizza at least once a week, she'd change up the crust and the sauces, but it made me feel good to know that she was doing it to make me happy. During her not so normal times, she would get annoyed by my vegetarianism and she made less of an effort to make me meals I'd enjoy. She would always bring up the fact that I've never eaten meat in my entire life.

She even told the story to strangers at the grocery store, "yes, it's the strangest thing you've ever seen", she'd recount in her sweet, lilting voice, "any time I'd try to feed her any type of meat, even blended with other things, she would just spit it out, and not just let it dribble down her chin, it was a violent projectile vomit sort of thing and it only happened when she ate meat, she never vomited or spit out anything else", and she'd laugh and shake her head. As much as I hated her telling the story, I knew it must be true. I feel intense revulsion any time I try to eat meat and IF I can make it cross my lips, my body rejects it immediately, so yes, it is the strangest thing, but easy, I just don't eat meat. When people ask me, I make it easy and don't tell the story that makes me sound like a freak baby, but just say it's because I love animals, and it's not a lie, because I do love them and would have chosen to be a vegetarian despite my eating oddity.

We were hanging out in the plaza, the boys were eating ice cream and making a mess. A couple of local boys came along on skateboards and were skating near us. I'm not sure why, but I went over to them and without speaking asked if I could borrow a board. I skated around a bit and on the way back to give it to them, I did a few tricks, did a few kick flips and a heel flip, I ollied on the curb and even did a frontside board slide on a bench. They clapped and I laughed as I handed them the board. They were complimenting me and patting me on the back with respect. My little brothers came running up and I pointed at them. They grabbed the boards offered up to them and they did their little show that they always practice, weaving in and out of each other's way, making figure eights as they crouched down on the boards. They threw in some backside 180s, I was impressed, that was a new trick they'd added. My little brothers really were amazing little prodigies. At this point the whole plaza was watching and some were taking pictures and video, including the guys who'd lent us the boards. The guys were cheering the little guys on and Luca and Ollie loved every minute.

We walked back to the hotel, my Dad looked tired, but he was beaming with pride, I could tell. He turned to me "You are so bold, sweets, so bold" chuckling to himself. I thought the pride was meant for the boys, but maybe it was for me too.

Phase Three

The beauty of Baja continued along in the third and final phase of our road trip. My Dad said there a lot of secret surf spots along the Baja, but that we would save them for another time, he was really excited to get "home".

After Loreto, the highway hugged the coast for a while even as we climbed through another mountain range. We stopped at a roadside lookout where you could see over the Gulf of California (also known as the Sea of Cortez). My Dad went to help the boys out of their seats when he noticed that Ollie had made a huge mess with a bag of Cheetos. He made Ollie stay in the car to help him clean it up and I took Luca to the edge where there was a wall and we could look out over the serene, mirror that was the sea that day. It was so peaceful. I sat cross-legged along the wall and Luca crawled into my lap and we looked out, I wondered what he was thinking.

"Sure looks nice down there, no waves, good for the stand-up paddle board". I should have known that's what he was thinking and he was right. It looked like a lake where you could paddle out to the distant islands without a ripple in the water. Just then, a little bird perched on my shoulder, it was a sweet little sparrow with a black throat. I reached over and offered him my finger and he stepped onto it and I showed him to Luca who squealed. "More Lily, more!!!!", he said.

I pet the little sparrow on the head showing Luca how to do it gently and suddenly there were four more, one on my knee, one on my shoulder, another on my arm and one on my head. "You're a bird lady Lily!", Luca laughed and laughed while the little sparrows played with our hair and nuzzled our faces. Then I heard my Dad close the car door and Ollie came running toward us and the little sparrows all flew off at once, but they didn't go far, I could feel them in the nearest bush.

I whispered to Luca, "Don't tell them about the birds, they're just ours, ok? They'll be jealous and we don't want them to feel bad." Luca nodded and climbed out of my lap to run and meet his twin. After some more photos, we continued.

After winding through the mountains a while longer, we came upon a long, straight, boring stretch that lasted for a few hours, I kept nodding off and I felt bad, knowing that my Dad was probably tired without anyone to help him drive. He stopped in the next little town to stretch his legs and get some caffeine. The boys were asleep so I stayed with them in the car. Next thing I know my Dad is opening the passenger side door and motioning me to get out. I got out and he said, "I need a little break" he said, and he tossed me the keys.
"But Dad?"

He shook his head, "Don't think about it, just do it, it's a long straight stretch for a while, let's see how you do". And just like that, I was driving! It felt amazing to be holding the wheel and pressing the gas, he wouldn't let me got too fast, but it was exhilarating, it felt powerful and I loved the feeling of control. I couldn't wait to tell my friends I was driving.

After about an hour he made me pull over and he drove again, which was good as we seemed to be getting into a curvier part of the road and there were more large trucks. "We're getting close, he said", as we entered a larger town, an actual city. La Paz was pretty cool, a great boardwalk along the bay, with sculptures, and lively restaurants and bars and such. We just took a walk along the malecon and enjoyed some cold lemonade. Fresh squeezed lemonade is very popular in Mexico; you can get it just about everywhere and it's so good. It's made with Mexican limes or limones and you can choose to have it made with sparkling or still water, both so good.

Back on the road, next stop the little art town of Todos Santos, where we had lunch, it was really a nice little town from what we could tell, but in reality, all we wanted was to reach our destination. We were tired. I felt like I was homeless and just living out of a suitcase. Logically I knew that it had really only been three days, but having packed up my old home and not knowing what my new home would be like, made me feel lost, and yes, a bit like a homeless wanderer.

"Okay guys, just a little while longer, less than an hour and we'll be there". I was so full from all the quesadillas I ate that I again started to nod off, but it seemed to last only a moment before my Dad was stopping at a toll booth to pay. "Okay, this is San Jose, your new town. We can explore later, let's find our house".

Chapter 8
Home

Right when you cross the border from the US into Mexico, it's a different feel. The smells are different, the sounds are different and even just on the surface, you can tell that the homes are different. I don't know how to describe the architecture and there are certainly exceptions, but in general, the neighborhoods seem, a bit, disorganized as though there had been no planning or forethought to where or how the houses would be built. I can also say that Mexican neighborhoods have flavor and personality. Their power lines may not be buried, but there are trees in the yards plentiful with mangos. There are no mailboxes and garbage bags hang on hooks on the telephone poles (so the dogs won't get into the trash I'm told), but the bougainvillea are trimmed and the patios are swept. People take pride in their homes and work around what they can't change. It's really a warm and inviting place.

Our new home was not far once we arrived in town. San Jose is a small city, with most of the modern conveniences, though maybe not all of what we are used to. Americans don't always realize just how convenient everything in the United States is, especially in big cities like San Diego where you can basically do anything and get anything at any hour, every day.

We went into our neighborhood and found our house. My Dad had seen it online and toured it "virtually" with the agent. He said it wasn't perfect, but it had everything we needed. The front door was open and when I asked about it, Dad said that we had a lady that would be helping us out and she came ahead to start cleaning and unpacking.

From the outside, all we could really tell was it was a two-story house with a garage and a nice patio out front, with two mango trees, various types of cactus, with a shade structure made of some interesting type of wood. It seemed like a normal house, even though it wasn't the same as US homes. It was bigger than our last house, at least the house part, our backyard was a bit smaller.

We walked in to boxes that my Dad had sent ahead, boxes and boxes and boxes, all over what would be our living room, but the kitchen and dining area were unpacked and ready and there was something that smelled wonderful on the stove simmering. We all ran upstairs to see what the bedroom situation was and that's where we found Elena. She was a small brown woman with a huge presence and a warm smile. She hugged me and the boys and kept saying, "Bienvenidos." She had been mopping and all the windows were open and the rooms were clean and it smelled fresh and clean. She grabbed my hand and told me to come with her. She started talking to me and I had to ask her to slow down so I could understand.

"This should be your room" she said. "It's not the largest room, but it has a bathroom and look…". She dragged me to the large window that had doors that opened onto a small balcony with one of the mango trees right in front of the balcony. It felt like you were in a tree. It was on the side of the house and the tree blocked out the neighbors and the street, it was perfect.

My Dad and the boys had larger rooms with an adjoining bathroom, and big built in closets. The boys would share the biggest one and my Dad would be in the one next to it. It's funny that this woman, who we just met, who we would all grow to love, had known exactly where to put us and what we needed. It was definitely a good sign.

We explored the downstairs which had a large living room, dining room, kitchen, pantry and another bedroom that my Dad would probably use as an office. He said that it was a rented house, but that we could paint our rooms and fix it up however we wanted. There was a dining room table and chairs already set up, but we had sold ours, so I wasn't sure where they came from, but they were nice and suited the house. Our bedroom furniture was in our rooms but disassembled. Dad decided he was too tired to build furniture and said that we'd have all day tomorrow to start setting up and that we should go to the beach. We all changed and got back in the car.

My Dad got in the car and looked at all of us. "What's with all the mopey faces?" and then he started laughing. "Don't worry, we're only driving for about four minutes and then you don't have to get back in the car until tomorrow, to go back to the house, I promise". He saw the relief in our faces, even Bilbo's and laughed again, we all laughed with him.

True to his word, we arrived in four minutes. "My buddy DJ has a condo here. He's out of town and said we could sleep here if we needed to and use his place when we want to come to this beach, there's also a pool and hot tub". His condo was on the fourth floor and looked right over the beautiful aqua blue waters of the Gulf of California. I flopped on the couch for a while before deciding to go for a swim, in the pool. I was too tired to fight currents, or paddle or anything. I just wanted to float in the pool with no cares in the world.

"This is nice Dad, relaxing, and not too hot," I said as I languished on the inflatable pool float I'd found at DJ's.

"Well it's only June, the real heat will be here soon, but it's only a few months, the rest of the year the weather is beautiful."

"I like my room".

"I'm glad Sweets".

"Dad?"

"Mmm?" he asked as he eased into the pool. The boys were running around in the grass with Bilbo and a soccer ball.

"How did you know we would like the house? Where did Elena come from? Where did the dining table come from, and why did you pick San Jose? I mean, you could have picked anywhere, why here? Have you been here before or …?"

"My sister, your Aunt Daniela."

I looked over at him and almost fell off my floaty thing. "Who????"

That night, my Dad and I sat on the couch, where he promised to tell me everything. Somehow I knew "everything" didn't really mean "everything", but I would take what I could get.

When I was little I used to ask my parents about their families and why I didn't have grandparents or cousins or uncles or aunts. My Dad would just shut down the conversation saying that his parents died when he was young and my Mom would change the subject and tell me a story, sometimes a French princess who didn't fit in, other times a girl who fell down a rabbit hole. Those were her go to stories anyway, there were more, but never the truth apparently.

"I have a sister, Daniela, she's a year and a half younger than I am. We grew up almost like twins. She's amazing, you'll love her and you'll meet her tomorrow".

"But where has she been? Why hasn't she ever visited? Why haven't I ever even heard about her?".

"Well it's difficult to explain Sweets, but I'll try. When you were born, my Mom and Dad and your Aunt Daniela all came to visit. It was a year after your Mom and I had gotten married and we were so in love, with each other and you. He smiled at the memory, but then his face went dark. My Mom would try to give your Mom advice, she was a new Mom and in Mexican families, the whole village helps to raise the child, so my Mom didn't feel like she was intruding. But your Mom took it really hard, she was having a hard time feeding you and you cried a lot and your Mom had to go off her medication so she wasn't very stable. This made things worse. The tension was high and your Mom ended up asking everyone to leave, it was a mess. After that, your Mom refused any input from anyone and she actually figured it all out on her own.

She said my parents were no longer welcome in our home and that I had to choose the new family I had created with your Mom or the family I'd grown up with. I didn't want to lose her or you, so I chose. Your Aunt Daniela was stubborn and kept coming around, at least once a year, but when you were around three, your mom and Daniela argued, I'm not sure about what exactly, but then she was banished too. At that point, I made a demand of my own. I told your Mom that she needed to choose our family too and that she needed to stay on her medications, which she didn't like to take, or else she would have to leave. She agreed, though she didn't always hold up her end of the deal. In fact, that's why she left us, she chose to live off medication, which I didn't agree with and she felt that was more important than staying a part of our family and raising her children."

He started to sound angry and hurt, so I didn't ask any more about my mother. In fact, I didn't want to hear about her. She was crazy and she chose herself, not us, so she was crazy and selfish and I didn't want to hear about her or think about her. I changed the subject.

"Do I have any cousins?", I asked hopefully.

"Yes, your aunt has a daughter, about a year older than you, her name is Catarina."

"Is she here? Will I meet her tomorrow? I can't believe this!"

"She's away at school, she's very smart and an incredible tennis player. She got a scholarship to a prestigious boarding school in Indiana, but I think she's in Ecuador or something right now".

She was so beautiful; I couldn't stop looking at her. From the moment she hugged me I knew she was a kindred spirit. I instantly loved her, so did the boys. In a way, I looked a lot like her, her hair was a shade darker than mine, but still a light brown and her eyes were a warm brown, where mine were green like my mother's, but the shape of the eyes was the same and we have the same high cheekbones. She had a small nose and mouth like me and her eyes drooped ever so slightly like mine, bedroom eyes they often call them. She was so happy to see us and meet the boys and she said she remembered me like it was yesterday. Apparently, all these years my Dad talked to her frequently, keeping it a secret from my mom. "Aunt Danni or Daniela, she said, I'm fine with whatever you want to call me." I was mesmerized, I thought she was the most wonderful person I'd ever met.

She came with gifts too. "Your Dad said you would probably want to paint your room".

"Yes, I was thinking a medium to dark periwinkle, but whatever, I'm pretty flexible."

She laughed and quickly left the room and came back with some paint cans. They were periwinkle, exactly what I was thinking! "How did you know?"

She shrugged, "I don't know, I just liked the color and hoped you might too."

The boys got a muted blue that would be perfect for them. She had bought us new comforters for our beds as well. Mine had trees and little birds on it, very Secret Garden. My Dad worked on the boys' room with them, putting together painting and putting together beds and Aunt Danni would help me in my room, which was nice, I really wanted to get to know her.

I found out a lot about her and my cousin Catarina. My aunt was the general manager of the Hilton Hotel here, which she said I could come and see anytime, swim in the pool, etc. We opened all the windows to let out the fumes and turned on the fans, I was starting to like how my room was coming together. While the paint dried, we started unpacking my clothes and other boxes.

"Still got the bird thing happening I see."

"What?", I asked, not having any idea what she was talking about.

She pointed to my balcony and all along the railing were little birds, perched along the edge. It was as if each neighborhood species had sent a representative. There was a woodpecker, a cardinal, an oriole, a sparrow, a wren, a dove, a finch, and a fluffy little bird I didn't immediately recognize, maybe it was a robin. All of them were just there, watching as my aunt and I painted, how long had they been there?

"What bird thing?", I asked, as though it was a totally normal thing to see on your balcony railing.

"The last time I visited you, you were almost three, and your mother was waging her own little war. She would ramble on about the birds and the birds in your room and more birds, it's never ending, and that crow, I'm gonna get that crow, she would say. I didn't really understand what she was talking about until I saw it for myself. I walked into your room one day, you'd just woken up from a nap. You weren't crying, but I heard you talking and I went to check on you and you were in your crib, we were actually building your big girl bed for your birthday, and in your crib, on your head, along the railing of your crib were a bunch of little birds, songbirds, all talking to you in their little chirps and songs. You were laughing and talking to them. When the birds saw me, one by one they flew out of the window, through a torn corner of the screen your Mom had put up. I grabbed you up and you told me "say by to my friends", in your sweet little voice, and you made me wave good bye. When I told your mom about it she was furious! I couldn't understand why some sweet little birds would make her so upset. She explained that there was constantly bird poop in your room and in your bed and even in your hair. She said that she'd put up a screen but that the birds just kept coming in. She finally figured out what was going on when she put a nanny cam in your room. There was a crow that would visit you for hours, almost like he watched over you and guarded you, and that he was the one that kept making holes in the screen".

I tried to laugh off the story, "hope I don't become a crazy bird lady who sits in the park and talks to the pigeons." I desperately hoped the birds on the rail would just go, I didn't want my aunt to think I was weird or crazy. Bilbo came bounding into the room at that moment and went straight to the balcony and started barking at the birds. They didn't budge, but looked at me instead and then seemed to start flying away, one by one.

Aunt Danni laughed and I think sensed I was uncomfortable so she dropped the subject and started arranging the fans so that the walls would dry quickly. We went and had some lunch, which Elena had made (my aunt Danni had apparently had a long discussion with her about my vegetarianism, and had purchased groceries with her so that she could make things I could eat) and we enjoyed a meal all together, laughing at the boys with blue paint all over them, they looked like Smurfs.

That was the first night we spent in our new home. Though I missed my friends, I did like my new room and I was ready for some adventure, everything that was part of the mundane in the states, would be different here, a new experience, and I decided to embrace it, as best I could. I texted the girls and said I'd video call them tomorrow to show them my new room and catch up.

Chapter 9
Welcome to Mexico

Whenever something happens that I'm not accustomed to, I just say to myself, "Welcome to Mexico".

When the garbage truck goes by picking up trash at 11:54 pm on a Tuesday, welcome to Mexico. When the water in the shower suddenly only trickles out, welcome to Mexico. When the grocery store doesn't have something normal, like bagels or sour cream, welcome to Mexico. When the restaurant is closed on a Sunday afternoon and the sign says it is open daily from 9-9, welcome to Mexico. When cars with loudspeakers go through the neighborhood selling water, or propane gas, or bread, or offer to buy your broken appliances at a great price, welcome to Mexico.

There are a lot of quirks and differences other than the obvious ones, but the people are friendly and no one seems to be in a hurry for anything. I'm getting accustomed to "Cabo time" it's not quite the punctuality I'm used to and I like it. You can tell the Americans at the grocery store right away. They are standing in the line, waiting to pay with their card or cash ready, tapping their feet, looking around not understanding what the hold-up is and the Mexicans are distinct because they have no sense of urgency. The cashiers are not rushing to make sure you are helped in a timely and efficient manner and the customers in line don't look impatient or annoyed, they are just going about life as usual. No sense of urgency, no rush, no hurry up we're late. Welcome to Mexico.

Those first few weeks were fantastic. We tried every restaurant and went to a new beach every day. We decided on our favorite places to eat and I learned that Cabo was actually pretty good as far as there being vegetarian and organic options. There are a lot of local organic farms and the veggies and fruit are abundant (though I hear that summer is the worst time of year for this because not too much grows in the heat down here). We discovered which beaches were good for snorkeling, kayaking, stand-up paddling, swimming and surfing. My Dad helped us scope out each spot and we reviewed the tides and the currents, the coves, reefs, rocks etc. I knew that he wanted to arm me with as much knowledge as he could because he wanted me to be able to go on my own, whenever I wanted. We went to the East Cape which is deserted in many areas and so beautiful and there is a marine reserve with a gorgeous reef there. We went to the Pacific Ocean side, which was a lot more what we were accustomed to with heavier waves and stronger currents, but the water was warm, definitely no wetsuits needed, which I loved of course.

About a month after we arrived, my father started working again. He was working with an environmental conservation group called Wild Coast, that works to preserve and protect the California coastline, from northern California to the coast of Baja. I guess he is their lawyer and he's licensed in California and Mexico, which is very useful for the group. Though he hasn't focused on environmental law before, he's been reading like crazy, since he first decided to move us here. The group's headquarters are in San Diego, in Imperial Beach to be more precise, where we used to live. They rented an office here and put him in charge of it, so he started to put together a team of mostly volunteers and sometimes people would come from the States as well to help out or if there was something special going on.

He said he would also be working with local organic farmers, helping them with any legal matters they may have. He worked a lot, but his schedule was flexible, not like it was before. He had time for us and he took charge of the boys, it wasn't my responsibility anymore. Because I didn't have to look after the boys, because Elena was a stable constant in our home, and because my friends were far away, I had a lot of time on my hands.

My Dad has a buddy, an ex-pat from Oklahoma who has been farming organically down here for years. We were invited to go see his farm and have dinner at his house. He's a really cool guy who knows about everything, has a million stories, and plays the guitar. He offered to teach me or my brothers if we want to learn, but more importantly, he has a daughter, Ruby, and she's my age. She's warm and friendly and quickly grabbed me and took me to her room to hang out. "Ugh, my Dad drives me crazy sometimes, it's just him and I, so I've heard all the stories and heard all his songs, my Mom lives in Santa Barbara and I go visit her, it's a 50/50 split, which is hard, because I have to homeschool, but this year I'm going to try and actually go to school, but I don't know where yet. Where are you going to go? Do you know anyone here? Do you like to go to the beach? Movies?".

I was bombarded by information and questions. I'm used to my friends, who know me better than I do, but I was happy to make a new friend and have someone here to hang out with. We decided to meet up tomorrow and go to the beach. Making plans with a friend definitely made me feel more welcome here and with a friend, maybe this could be my home.

Chapter 10
Sunshine

Once I met Ruby, summer break really kicked in for me. I had a home that was interesting and new and I was at a point where the warm days ran into each other. I wasn't thinking about my Mom every moment any more, I tried hard not to think about her at all. When Ruby asked me about my Mom, I told her I didn't have one and that I didn't want to talk about it. She nodded and never asked about it again. Ruby was entertaining and so welcoming, she always wanted to make people feel at ease. She asked a lot of questions, but instinctively knew when not to pry, she respected my privacy and understood I was guarded, but still wanted to be my friend. Ruby knew everyone in town pretty much and liked introducing me. She was dying to introduce me to some guy that she thinks I will just love. Apparently, he's in Europe for the summer and is the best friend of the guy she likes, who is in Guadalajara visiting family or something. We went to the beach almost every day, we went to the movies, hung out in the plaza eating churros, letting Bilbo run around. Sometimes her Dad lent her the car and sometimes my Dad let me drive his car.

I loved driving. There aren't as many rules in Mexico. Basically, watch out for everyone else and don't hit anyone or anything. I'm sure there are actual rules that I'll have to memorize when I go get my license, but there's nothing like learning by doing! My Dad just made sure I wasn't driving far and that if I happened to get stopped, I'd speed dial him and pin my location. So far I haven't needed it, I've only needed a little courage and a destination.

I saw my Aunt Danni almost every day, though she worked a lot at the hotel. I guess being the GM of a nice hotel is no small feat, she worked hard for many years and rose through the ranks. And she's a woman, not very many women have such high-ranking jobs in Mexico, though I hear it's slowly changing. I was lucky that I could visit her at the hotel whenever I wanted, I could use the pool and I had access to a nice little cove just down the beach. It was also 12 minutes from home, so my Dad would let me drive there.

These were my summer days, spent sometimes at the pool at the Hilton, sometimes the beach with Ruby, or the movies, sometimes the beach with the boys and my Dad, it was very hot, but there was plenty to do. I also often went kayaking with Bilbo. My Dad's friend DJ, with the condo at Las Olas, on the beach, let me stash my kayak in his storage and let me use his extra parking space. The security guy knew me and let me through the gate with a wave.

Today Ruby was busy helping her Dad and I decided to go to the beach with Bilbo. I took an umbrella, a book, my hat, a towel, a little ice chest with a couple of bottles of water and some quesadillas and some dog treats. I have a little portable water bowl for him too and I make sure it's always in my beach bag. We got to the beach at Las Olas and I dragged the kayak out of storage. I set up my little spot on the beach and went out on the kayak. Bilbo almost always goes on the kayak with me. He's not the best swimmer, but he loves the kayak, and even when I jump off to snorkel or just cool off, he'll watch the water patiently, standing guard until I climb back in, he's pretty cute.

I paddled out to a rock that's a surf spot for the locals, I positioned myself so I wasn't in their way, but I could still take a few pictures. The surfing conditions weren't ideal and I soon got bored because no one was catching anything. I paddled around to see if there were any sea turtles. I've seen one particular turtle near this rock a few times, he seems to be here in the afternoons, so maybe I was too early. We paddled back to shore and I pulled the kayak up to my beach camp and then went back to the water for a quick dip to cool off. When I got out, Bilbo was faithfully guarding the camp and I gave him some water and treats. I just sat for a while, taking in the beauty of the turquoise waters and decided to stay all afternoon and just soak it in. I pulled out my book and started to relax.

After about an hour, which included an unexpected nap, I went back in for a swim. I noticed a group of kids my age, taking turns on a skim board and messing around. There were three guys and a girl. The girl seemed a little younger, like maybe one of their younger sisters, tagging along because "Mom said so". I got out of the water and observed them from the shade of my umbrella. I was far enough away that I could watch them without them noticing, but I couldn't hear everything they were saying. Really, I was watching one of them in particular. I couldn't keep my eyes off of him. He was a Golden God! His brown hair bleached by the sun, tan and slim, but muscled in all the right places. Basically every muscle was defined and he was obviously a surfer (I'm an expert at detecting them) and his smile, when he smiled I think I melted and it wasn't even a smile meant for me. He had a dimple on one side and his chin was dimpled too. His hair was not short but not too long either, chin length maybe, it was hard to tell as it was wet and sandy. I just couldn't stop looking. I dared for one second to wish that I could meet him and half a second later, Bilbo took off, he just started running down the beach, he looked like he was on a mission.

"Bilboooooo", I yelled, "Bilboooo come back here", I stood up and yelled for him a few more times. Of course, he was heading straight for the kids, straight for the Golden God, oh how embarrassing! What was he doing? Bilbo jumped on Mr. Golden and started licking him, happily barking as if he was a long-lost friend.

I adjusted my bathing suit and dusted the sand off and headed toward them to fetch my stupid, embarrassing dog. I walked up to them, feigning cool, collected, confidence "Hi, sorry about that, he's normally very obedient, not sure what got into him", I said, with a big stupid grin on my face.

"Well it must be because we're cousins, isn't that right Bilbo?" he looked at Bilbo, who he was now holding and scratched him on the head. He laughed and noticed I didn't understand, "I'm Emilio, Emilio Baggins", he said and put out his hand for me to shake.

"Nice to meet you Emilio, Baggins? Really?", I asked. "I'm Lily, and I didn't mean to be rude, it's just an uncommon name".

"Not for hobbits!" he laughed, "but for humans, I suppose it is, it was Baginsky at some point, changed at Ellis Island I think."

"Well I like it, it reminds me of a hobbit and I like hobbits". What an idiot, did I just say that?

"You must, you named your dog after one. So what, do I look like a hobbit? I kinda hope I do since you like them so much".

"I like that they're loyal and steadfast, sturdy, curious yet hesitant, and no you certainly don't look like a hobbit and thank you for holding my dog" I rambled. I felt like a total idiot and needed to get away quickly before the Golden God melted me into a puddle with those thick eyelashes and dreamy eyes that seemed to laugh and sparkle whenever he did.

"Well I didn't have a choice, he practically jumped into my arms, but he's a cute little guy, and after all we are cousins". He gave Bilbo's head another scratch and handed him over.

I mumbled thanks again and put Bilbo down on the sand and told him to go back to our spot and stay and he happily trotted back, while I followed wondering if Mr. Golden thought I was a total moron.

Just as I got back to my spot where I planned to bury myself in the sand and disappear, I was tapped on the shoulder.

"Hey Lily" he was slightly out of breath from running, was he running after me? How odd.

"Yeah?"

"Can we share your camp spot?", he asked and grinned ear to ear. How could I say no to that? WHY would I say no to that?

"Sure, make yourselves at home" and they did. One of the boys was his brother Theo, the other his cousin Alonzo and his sister Alexa.

The boys dumped their stuff and left the girls to watch their stuff. Now I understand why they came over, they needed a friend for Alexa and someone to watch their stuff. Alexa was two years younger than me and a competitive swimmer. She talked a mile a minute and was very competitive, I could tell, I'm sure having two older brothers made her that way. Though I wouldn't want to face her in the pool, she was pleasant to be around. She dominated the conversation, which was fine with me, I preferred to listen. She told me about their family, Emilio is the oldest (a year older than I am), Alonzo, "Al" she called him, And Theo were my age and she was thirteen, though I must say, she was a very mature thirteen.

When the boys came back, Alexa scolded them, "we said we'd be back by six to help make dinner, Mom is not gonna be happy, she needs the car to go buy the stuff". They started packing up their things and Emilio pulled his phone out of his backpack.

"It was great to meet you Lily, hope to see you here again", Alexa said politely.

"Hey Lily" his voice made my skin tingle. I turned towards him, hoping not to get swallowed up in that gaze, rendered speechless.

"What's your full name?", he asked.

"Lily Louise Balea" I responded. He smiled and I was done. Yep, puddle on the ground, someone was going to have to mop me up.

He handed me his phone, "Is that how you spell it?" I nodded. "Can you put your phone number in there?", he asked. Without hesitation, I did. "You live here?". I nodded again. "Okay, why don't you go home now, I'm going to call you in about an hour". I couldn't say anything. I didn't know what to say really. I just waved as they left and packed up my stuff and went home.

Of course I couldn't stop thinking about the Golden God. Why did he take my number? Was he being polite because I watched his stuff and talked to his sister? Why was I told to go home, isn't that a bit arrogant considering he just met me?

I'm sure he doesn't know I don't like being told what to do. But still, I kinda wanted to go home and wait for his call, even though my cell phone was in my hand and I didn't need to be home when he called. The rebel in me decided not to go home and stay at the beach instead and read my book. Of course, I couldn't concentrate for an hour. The minutes ticked by so slowly, I couldn't read, I couldn't eat, I didn't even notice the pelican sitting a foot from me until Bilbo barked to get my attention. I had to laugh, I'm not sure what I'd do without Bilbo, his little black, smushed-in face was such a comfort to me in any situation. I scratched his head and told him to be quiet so the large pelican would come closer. I took a few photos of the awesome bird, he even spread his wings for me and let me give him a pat on the head and back, he enjoyed it too. Just as I was going to tenderly touch his beak and pet him again, my phone rang. The bird jumped back when I suddenly dove for my phone. It was him. Do I answer? Of course I was going to answer, but I did let it ring a few times, trying to play it cool.

"Hello?"

"Hi Lily, it's Emilio, you home?"

"No, I'm still at the beach, I got caught up taking photos of a really cool pelican". I must sound like such a dork.

"Aw man, I was hoping you'd be home so we could hang out for a few minutes before I have to go make dinner with my family, they're waiting at home for the groceries, we're going to grill some steaks if you'd like to join us." Did he sound disappointed that I wasn't home?

"I'm a vegetarian" I said, dumbfounded at the invitation, once again rendered speechless.

"Oh, okay, that's good to know" he said cheerfully, "um, we will have other stuff to eat".

"I'm sorry" I said, "that didn't come out right, I don't mean I can't come because I'm a vegetarian, I actually have plans for dinner with my family too, at a new farm to table restaurant that grows all of their own stuff and it's all organic, and we've had it planned for a while and I don't feel like I can bail on them" I rambled.

"No worries" he said, "I'll call you tomorrow, enjoy your dinner".

He hung up. Was he mad or was he disappointed? He couldn't have been disappointed, could he?

I packed up my stuff, threw everything in the kayak and dragged it up the beach to the storage space at Las Olas and then drove home.

I got there before the boys and Dad, and Elena wasn't there because we were going out for dinner and had the night off. There was a pot with purple calla lilies on my doorstep. They were so pretty and I already knew they would be perfect on my balcony, but where had they come from? Was my Dad here, I didn't see his car?

Then I noticed a note taped to the side. It was handwritten:

Lily Louise,
I thought of you when I saw these. I really enjoyed meeting you today. I was hoping you'd be home so I could ask you in person, please call me so I can ask you out on a date.
-E

My knees actually went a little weak, I had to sit down. I sat there for a little while, just holding the potted lilies on my lap. Was this really happening? The Golden God wants to go out on a date with ME??? Again, Bilbo saved me, he started nudging me with his wet nose, he really wanted to go inside and eat, he was so hungry. "Sorry buddy, let me get you food, you're getting another treat today too", he practically did backflips he was so excited and it helped me focus on something else for a minute and regain the strength in my legs.

I found an old wooden crate in the garage and took it up to my room. I placed in on the balcony and put the lilies on top of it to give them a little more height and reach the sun for part of the morning. I took a photo and sent it to Emilio with a caption that said, thank you, I love them, they're beautiful.

He responded with a simple "You're welcome, call me after dinner".

Ugh. I knew my dinner would be ruined because the Golden God would be consuming my every thought. My heart was already beating in anticipation of the phone call later.

Dinner was amazing, so fresh and so yummy. They had a ton of vegetarian options and the farm was beautiful. They had all sorts of animals, dogs running around, parrots, and even lemurs, but my head was filled with Emilio and I didn't even notice that the entire pack of dogs sat next to my chair during dinner, my aunt pointed it out and I shrugged "they must smell Bilbo", and the dreamy stupor I was in continued.

As we were walking out the door, one of the parrots screeched, "Lily, Lily, bye Lily". Everyone turned to the bird, but me.

"I think someone is in love", Dad said laughing.

"WHAAAT?", I said, much too loudly.

"The bird Lily, it's calling your name", he said pointing at it.

I laughed. Geez, what an idiot. I looked at my Aunt Danni and she smiled, an all too knowing smile, she knew something was up.

I couldn't bring myself to call him, just sent him a quick text saying, "Home from dinner, it was awesome", and attached a photo of the salad and fresh pasta I had. I also included a photo that the waiter took of all of us. I anxiously awaited a text. My phone rang.

"Hello?"

"What's up with the dogs?"

"What dogs?"

"In the picture, with your family, there's a pack of dogs all sitting up, staring at you, I've never seen anything like that before".

I cringed, thank goodness he couldn't see my mortified face.

"Hahaha" I laughed disingenuously, "I was giving them some treats I had in my bag, Bilbo's treats, not my treats, you know, I always have his stuff with me, and they were so cute and I was feeding them", again, I rambled like an idiot, and to top it all off I'm a terrible liar, so I'm sure I sounded like a double idiot.

"Hmmm, I'm not sure I buy that, they almost look like they are listening to your thoughts, not waiting for a treat".

"What? Haha, okay, sure, that's what's happening" I said sarcastically. Crap. Change the subject now.

"I really loved the lilies, I've never seen calla lilies that color before."

"I saw them and just thought that you needed to have them."

We talked for at least an hour, about our families, our homes, school, everything. He lives in San Diego, in Ranch Bernardo, kind of a ritzy area and we've surfed in a lot of the same spots, it's crazy that we've never met before. His family has a condo here, near Las Olas where my Dad's friend lives (and I store my kayak) and they are here every school vacation. His Dad is also a corporate lawyer like my Dad, we don't know if they know each other, but I would imagine they might. We had a lot in common as far as sports and water and art. He says his family has been coming here since he was three.

"Since you are new to town, I'd like to show you some special spots that I like, what do you think?"

"Well I think you are asking me out on a date and if that's true, then I think I would love that". I said, summoning the courage to say what I was really thinking.

"It's a date then, how about tomorrow, I can't wait".

He can't wait? Me neither. I was jumping in the air and kicking my feet together in my mind.

"Until tomorrow then."

"All right, I'll put together a plan and talk to you in the morning" and he hung up.

Then a text: Sweet dreams Lily Louise, I'm really glad we met, say thanks to cousin Bilbo.

I called the girls immediately but I could only get a hold of Summer. I told her the whole story and she asked a million questions. She laughed, "I'm so glad you finally like someone, I was starting to worry you were frigid and loveless, or maybe gay and struggling with the truth". She laughed playfully and begged for more details. "I'm only joking, you know that right? I know you don't let your guard down for just anyone. He must be special, I'm super happy for you".

"Who are you happy for and why", I heard Sophie's loud voice in the background.

"Oh here," Summi said, "the girls are here, tell them the story". They reacted pretty much exactly like Summi did, but

Eva didn't say much, though I could hear her nodding and smiling. They wanted every detail after tomorrow's big date.

"Stop calling it a BIG date", I said, "it makes me uncomfortable or embarrassed or pressured or something".

They laughed at me and after an important discussion on what I should wear on this non-BIG date, we said goodnight.

I missed them so much, but thinking about the Golden God eased the sting a bit.

Chapter 11
The BIG date

He was picking me up at 5:00. I had already talked to the girls and we'd planned what I should wear. Because it's so hot here, options are limited, so we chose a cute sundress, a pretty purple shade, similar to the lilies he'd given me. I called Ruby and told her about the Golden God and everything that had happened. I thought maybe she knew him because their family comes so often, but she didn't seem to know him. She made me promise to let her know all about it tomorrow.

I didn't know how to tell my Dad I was going on a date, so I just said I was having dinner with new friends. It helped that Emilio's family lives in the condos next to Las Olas and they know his friend DJ, so he didn't really ask too many questions after that. I waited downstairs so that there wouldn't be any awkward Dad/Guy meeting at the door. He knocked and I rushed to open the door but Ollie was there before me.

"Who is it?", his little voice asked through the door.

"Emilio"

"Sorry I don't know you, go away."

"No wait, I'm here for Lily".

I opened the door with an awkward smile and yelled up to my Dad, "Leaving Dad".

"Keep your phone with you and not too late Sweets," he yelled back from upstairs. I was happy that he was busy working and was distracted. I couldn't tell if he was oblivious to the fact that I was going on a date or if he was purposely giving me space so it wouldn't be awkward, it didn't matter, I secretly thanked him and practically ran out the door before he decided to come down and investigate.

We got in the jeep and Emilio was beaming that smoldering smile at me, I was determined not to be an idiot, but he wasn't going to make it easy.

"Hi" I said, trying my best not to look like a grinning fool.

"Hi" he said, "was that Ollie who opened the door, or didn't open the door really?", he laughed.

"Yes, how did you know?"

He shrugged, "I guessed, but you did say that he's the more assertive one of the two". Wow, he actually listened to me and remembered details about my family. I don't even remember saying that, but I must have because he did ask me a lot about my family when we talked on the phone. What I didn't tell him about was my Mom. I just told him I didn't have a mother; it was fairly recent and I didn't want to talk about it. I especially didn't tell him that she's crazy and that I might be as well.

We were talking and laughing for about five minutes before I even asked where we were going.

"Have you been to the marina?", he asked.

"I've been to the one in Cabo San Lucas, but not the one here in San Jose."

"Okay, good, then I get to show you some cool stuff, we can also eat there, there are a few restaurants, but I chose the one that has most vegetarian options."

"It's really considerate of you, I appreciate it, but you don't have to worry about that, I always figure something out, I hate for people to go out of their way because of my eating preferences."

"Well when you are trying to impress someone and get them to like you, you go out of your way to make sure they are happy."

Speechless.

"Lily?"

"Sorry, I just don't know what to say, and rather than say something dumb, I just kept quiet, but now that I'm listening to what I'm saying, I still sound dumb even though I was trying not to."

He laughed again, "I'm not laughing at you, I promise, you're just, just, so genuine, and I really never know what you are going to say. I love that you can be super quiet one minute and rambling the next."

I couldn't help but smile, wide. He shook his head, mumbled "beautiful" I think, and returned his focus to driving. I already missed looking at his eyes and smile, so I concentrated on his hair, shoulders, and hands, then he reached over with his free hand and held mine, squeezing it for reassurance. I put my other hand over his and just watched him, enjoying the ride, ignoring the scenery as nothing could compare to this Golden God at my side.

We arrived at Puerto Los Cabos, the marina here in San Jose. I'd never been. I'd only been to the more touristy one in Cabo San Lucas. There were definitely no crowds here, not many people at all, which was nice.

"There are some really cool sculptures here, all around the marina. I figured we could walk around and check them out and then maybe grab a bite to eat."

He got out and walked around to my side of the jeep. I'd already opened the door and he rushed over to help me out of the car. Obviously I can get out of a car by myself, but any excuse for his electrifying touch was welcomed. He held my hand and led me toward the path along which were some amazing sculptures by a female surrealist artist named Leonora Carrington. He paused at the first one along the path. It's ironic that we were there to look at some surrealist art because this date was surreal. I floated along as if in a dream, I couldn't feel my feet touching the ground, I think every butterfly from within ten miles was fluttering around in my belly. I soon forgot to be self-conscious, I soon forgot to overanalyze every word and situation. We seemed to fit seamlessly, expressing our thoughts without filters or fear of judgement, laughing easily, and comfortably allowing silence when words were not necessary.

We took photos of our favorite sculptures and took photos of each other and some together. Some were very silly and lighthearted and when I would look back on them, as I would come to often, we seemed almost ethereal, like our souls were light and happy.

Some of the sculptures were actually quite dark and evoked other emotions, but not even they could damper our good moods. We found a statue we loved, it was a goat, but a goat given human traits, wearing a robe, seemingly imparting his knowledge to others. He looked like he was philosophizing or telling a story to his students and followers. He looked wise and wizard-like, almost like the Dumbledore of the animal world, or Goat Gandalf. "What are you thinking?", Emilio asked.

"Well I think Goat Gandalf here might be my favorite of all the sculptures." I felt Emilio's eyes on me and I turned to look at him. He wasn't smiling his usually melty grin, he looked more serious.

"What's wrong?", I asked, trying to figure out if I'd said something stupid or offensive.

"Nothing" he said, almost a whisper, "nothing at all", and he took my face in his hands and kissed me. I closed my eyes and stopped thinking and just let the moment overtake me. When he started to pull away, I wrapped my arms around his neck and pulled him back.

When we stopped, we didn't let go. He put his forehead on my forehead and I felt him smiling.

"That was amazing" I said, no slobbery mess like before, this was so different, soft and sweet, and let's face it, there were some major fireworks going off through my whole body, I was worried that I might be shaking.

He hugged me tight and then gave me another quick kiss on the lips, "Yes it was" and he helped me up off the bench. We kept walking hand in hand, talking about where we should eat and other things, but honestly, I couldn't stop thinking about that kiss and when we could do it again.

The sculptures came to an end at the boats in the marina but the path kept curving around.

"I think if we follow the path it'll lead to that bridge and we can head over to that restaurant", he pointed. I'm not sure why but I suddenly started to feel queasy and odd, with a sense of dread, the exact opposite of what I'd been feeling all afternoon. I was especially sad that the euphoria was being hijacked by this discomfort.

We reached the bridge and I felt a stabbing pain in my stomach, like nothing I'd ever felt, it paralyzed me and I couldn't take another step.

"What's up?", the Golden God looked at me and his face changed, perhaps because mine had, and perhaps because there were tears streaming down my face and I couldn't control them.

The pain became increasingly worse and thought I was being stabbed repeatedly in the abdomen, over and over, and over, the pain dropped me to my knees and I started to hear voices. Soon the pain overtook me and the world seemed to go black.

"The baby, they took the baby, why, where's my baby", I screamed, "they took my baby, I need help, please, my baby, my baby, where are they taking her?"

I briefly opened my eyes and saw that Emilio was looking at me, trying to hold me and figure out what was wrong, but he also kept looking over his shoulder, something else was going on and it was distracting him, he looked so confused.

Again, the stabbing, horrible, unbearable pain, I started puking my guts out, violently and then again the world went black.

"Noooooooo, noooooo, please, please, the baby, please," I was whimpering, cradled in Emilio's arms. He was holding me and trying to wipe my tears and my face and my forehead with a cool cloth. I started to come back and I noticed he was wiping me with his shirt. He'd taken it off and poured water on it I guess. I didn't really know what was happening. He picked me up and I put my arms around his neck and let him carry me back to the car. He put me in the seat and buckled me in. He gave my face a final, gentle wipe and went around to the other side and got in.

"I'm sorry, I don't know…", my voice trailed off. He grabbed my hand and squeezed it.

"You're going to be okay," he reassured me, "your color is coming back, I'll take you home so you can rest and feel better."

I looked at him and he looked, grim? How could this wonderful, magical, amazing day end like this? I couldn't bear to see the Golden God like this, I looked away and stared out the window all the way home.

My Dad was waiting at the door to help me inside. Had Emilio called him?

"She's looking better now," he said to my Dad, as though they've always known each other.

"Thank you," he replied as he helped me out of the car and up the stairs. They shook hands and Emilio left. He didn't say good bye I thought. And I started to cry again, I just found him and now he's gone.

My Dad hugged me and took me up to my bed. "Here's some cool water to drink and some clean clothes (pajamas), do you need help?". I shook my head.

"I'll be okay, I'm sure whatever it was is out of my system now. I hope I didn't throw up all over him, how embarrassing".

My Dad laughed, "I wouldn't worry about that Sweets, everything is going to be okay, get some rest and let me know if you need anything."

"Dad?"

"Yes?"

"I wasn't drinking, but I feel like I did".

He chuckled again, "I know Sweets, drink plenty of water, you're probably dehydrated".

Chapter 12
The Plan

Later that night my Dad brought me some dinner and more water and I got up and took a quick shower, only to go straight back to my bed. I called the girls but only found Eva. I told her everything and she was so happy for me. She didn't seem to think the whole puking thing was a problem and that he'd be calling at any time now to check on me and I should just wait it out.

I later found Summi who loved the first part of the story but thought that I should text him and apologize and that it could definitely be a deal breaker. "Um, he's a guy, he's not gonna want to deal with a crazy girl who screams and cries and pukes. But you can fix it, just text him and say you're sorry and that you got some crazy food poisoning or something".

I decided to wait to hear what Sophie thought before I did anything and maybe Ruby too.

I fell asleep for a while and when I woke up, I had a text, from him. "Hope you are feeling better."

I didn't know what to say or if I should respond at all. I tried Sophie again and told me what to do in her sweet, bossy way.

"Just keep it simple, hopefully this will all blow over". She reassured me and I could tell she was trying really hard not to ask me a million questions about what really happened to me. She controlled herself as best she could.

"Can I please just ask one question?", she asked, I could almost hear her cringing over the phone.

"Ok".

"Was it similar to the incident that we aren't supposed to ever mention again?".

"Sort of, yes".

"Okay, well, rest up and I'll talk to you tomorrow".

I appreciated that she didn't pry more than that, which took quite a bit of restraint for the uber curious Sophie.

I decided to text him back.

"Thank you for everything, I'm feeling better, but tired".
I drifted off to sleep with the phone in my hand, he didn't text back that night.

Two days since the BIG date and no phone call or text. I can't understand why he wouldn't reach out, well, that's not true, I totally understand why, I guess I just hoped that because the beginning of the date was so incredible, that maybe he'd overlook the disaster in which it ended. I've always been a bit hopeful, but since my Mom left, I've kept all hope hidden away in that little box in the back of my mind and now I've built a wall around it.

When I did get the communication I so desperately desired, it wasn't exactly what I'd wished it would be and I had to initiate the contact.

"Hi, I'm sorry for your barfy shirt."

Nothing for a long time, then:

"I'm trying to understand what happened. I'm so sorry".

WHAT? WHAT does that mean???? I guess he's sorry he met me? Is he sorry because he can't be with a crazy freak like me? Is he sorry he ever asked me out? I was distraught, how could this be happening. What happened to me? What were those voices? Why did they have to come during the perfect date? Should I be taking medicine? Do I need to go to a doctor? I decided not to think about the details and to just be sad. My heart was broken, I didn't even get a chance to love him.

That week was torturous, but I did my best not to think about it. I went to the hotel pool with my book every day. My aunt made me laugh and brought me veggie burgers and sweet potato fries she had the chef make for me. On her day off she said she wanted to spend the day with me and the boys. We went and had lunch in San Lucas and then took the boys to an arcade.

"I'm ready to go, I've had enough of this arcade" I tried to say without too much melancholy, "we could go chill on the beach?"

"Actually, we are meeting your Dad at the beach in San Jose, the one by the estuary. He has some special project going on there that he says we need to see".

We dragged the boys off the mini basketball, where a crowd had gathered to watch these little guys never miss a shot, and headed to meet Dad.

We parked and right away I started to feel better. In fact, walking down the path toward the beach, I felt a huge smile plastered on my face and I think I was humming! All of a sudden, I felt a pulling in my chest. Not a painful thing, impossible to describe, but it's like my heart wanted to get somewhere quick and it was pulling me forward, but it wasn't painful, it was joyous! I broke into a run, though I didn't know where I was running, I only felt which direction to go. Then I saw a huge white canopy, several tents put together to create a large shaded space and I knew that's where I had to go. I saw my Dad waving at us but it wasn't him I was running towards. When I reached the tent, I saw hundreds and hundreds of newborn sea turtles. They were everywhere, at various stages, some still breaking out of their shells, others walking around, testing their new, paper thin fins. I immediately picked up a few and let them crawl in my hands,

I felt such wonder and joy, they emanated newness and a special euphoria that I can only imagine is the euphoria of being born into the world. Needless to say, I felt incredible and my whole body was buzzing with electricity. After I realized that I was sitting in the middle of the canopy with baby turtles crawling all over me, for quite some time apparently, I gingerly put all the turtles down and went to say hi to my Dad.

"How come you never told me about this Dad?"

"It was my first time protecting sea turtle eggs and I didn't know if the project would be successful, we still have to make sure they get to the ocean safely."

"I'm going to help Dad, I have to, we have to wait until the seabirds have finished eating, probably just after sunset and if it's cloudy, which it seems it won't be, then we have to shine a light over the ocean so they can see where to go, but we can't let them get confused by other lights and go the wrong way, they need to see the horizon, and", my Dad touched my arm so I would stop talking.

"Yes, we were going to wait until after sunset and yes, you can help".

We sat and watched the turtles and planned the release. We had all brought our suits and I decided to check the water out and see where the best release spot would be. Releasing them directly in front of their nests was ideal, I guess their mothers knew best. There was a nearby cove that helped keep the wave action minimal and there didn't seem to be too many natural predators in the water, but there were a lot of birds circling the area.

After sunset, we waited and waited, but the birds didn't seem to want to leave. Of course the birds knew what was under that canopy and they were waiting for their chance at a feast, they only had to wait for the humans to leave or let their guard down. It wasn't looking good for the infant turtles. We made sure any lights near us were off so they wouldn't be confused, the closest hotel turned off its lights in order to help, though developments like the hotel are a huge problem, they are ruining the natural habitats of so many animals.

The boys came running up to me and were pulling on my shirt to get my attention.

"WHAT?"

"We have an idea for the turtles", Ollie said.

"Take the birds away Lily!", Luca said too loudly, overexcited about their brilliant idea.

"Shhhh, not so loud", I kneeled down to talk to them closely and quietly. "Now, what do you want?".

"You're the bird lady Lily". Luca said.

Ollie rolled his eyes, "You can take the birds away with your magic and we can let the turtles go".

I laughed, "I left my magic wand at home, so I don't think I can make them disappear".

"Lily, you can walk over there" Ollie pointed east.

"And the birds will follow you" Luca finished.

I can't believe I agreed to try the plan of six year olds, but why not try, at least they would be happy. I told them not to say anything until they noticed the birds were gone, then they needed to tell Dad it was time, if he didn't notice the birds were gone. IF they were gone, I was wishing I had some bird seed or something.

I tried to leave the camp as inconspicuously as possible and I meandered down the beach. I didn't know what to do, I just hoped they'd follow. I wished in my head, please, please, please birds, just follow me for a while. I kept walking and praying that they'd follow. Just as I was cursing myself for being a moron, I turned around and saw, birds, every bird in the area it seemed like. It was pretty intimidating, like the movie *The Birds*, I started to get a little scared that all these birds were following me? But when I took some deep breaths, I realized I didn't really feel scared, at all, the birds weren't hostile and they weren't really even coming near me, almost like they were forming a protective barrier, my own little security team. I didn't stop to think what they thought they were protecting me from, I just kept walking and walking, as far from the baby turtles as possible. I cleared my mind and made sure NOT to think about the turtles. I just tried to breathe and be in the moment, clearing my mind with each breath. I stayed away until I felt something, something else. A new feeling, it was like what it feels like to be fresh and new and free. I knew then that the turtles were swimming in the ocean. They were still in danger of crabs and other unseen forces, but I'd cleared the area as best I could and I just hoped that as many as possible would make it to maturity and we'd meet sometime in the ocean or maybe when they came back to lay their own eggs.

I told the birds to go home and they did, at least I think they did. I walked back to the turtle camp and saw so many happy people, hugging and laughing and smiles all around. The boys ran and hugged me.

"You did it, you did it" they repeated in little sing song voices.

"Shhh, I said, no talking about the magic". I winked and hugged them back.

As we were leaving my Aunt Danni said, "You missed the release".

I shrugged and smiled, "No I didn't."

It had been over a week since the last text from Emilio. I didn't want to think about it, so I kept busy. I mostly went to the hotel so that I wouldn't accidentally run into him. It would break me if I saw him. It would be awkward; I wouldn't know what to say. I've always guarded my feelings and when my Mom left, I cemented them shut, but the Golden God didn't seem to care about the cement wall, he was just himself and I had let him in. I immersed myself in books and the pool and playing with the boys and Bilbo. Ruby was in Santa Barbara but would be back soon, maybe I'd be ready to talk about what happened then.

I was at the beach in front of the Hotel when my phone rang. My phone rarely rang, I usually just got texts, so I was surprised to hear it. Then I saw, it was him, I didn't know if I should answer, but I really wanted to, so I did.

"Hi," he said, "I've missed you". I definitely wasn't expecting that. I MISSED YOU, I wanted to yell.

"Hi" was all I could say. I didn't want to be the one to fill the silence, I wanted him to talk.

"I'm sorry I haven't called, I needed to figure everything out."

"And did you? Figure everything out?", I replied, perhaps there was a snarky tone to my voice, but what exactly did he need to figure out? Whether he liked me or not? Whether or not he could deal with the crazy?

"Well, I needed to understand what happened and I think I do and then I needed to do some research and come up with a plan".

"A plan, what are you talking about?" Was he going to send me to a psychiatrist and he had to research the right one? I didn't like where this conversation was going.

"Listen, I'm not going to a doctor or anything like that, I feel better and I'm sure I'll be fine, and I don't need people knowing what happened the other day, I like to keep things private and I wouldn't want to worry my Dad and",

"Wait, hold on," he interrupted my ramble, I could tell he was trying not to laugh.

"What?" I said completely annoyed. This guy was dumping me and sending me to a psychiatrist? I don't think so.

"I think you are misunderstanding me, I'm sorry, I'm not being very clear, I have a lot to tell you. I'm coming over, are you home?"

"No, I'm at the beach in front of the Hilton".

"Don't move, I'll be there in ten minutes".

It was ten minutes of pure torture. I tried to meditate. I didn't want to try and predict what he would say.

He strolled down the beach in all his Golden God glory, my breath caught in my throat and the butterflies in my belly woke up and decided to have a party. Then he saw me and flashed me that smile. I couldn't get up off my towel, I just sat there and waited for him to come to me, I knew my legs wouldn't work if I did try and stand.

"Can I sit with you?"

I motioned for him to have a seat, not trusting my voice. I wanted to cry.

"You look so sad, why are you so sad?" he asked as he reached up and caught a tear that I was desperately trying to hold in, "no, no, don't cry," and he hugged me and stroked my hair, I melted into him, holding back my tears, determined not to cry and to enjoy his touch as long as it would last. He pulled back, "I have a lot to tell you, I think it's going to make you happy, it's what I've been working on all week".

I shook my head, "I have no idea what you are talking about, you haven't called or texted and I acted crazy and maybe I am crazy and you came here to dump me and", I stopped my ramble when he shook his head and laughed.

"I'm sorry, I'm not laughing at you, at least not like that, I just really, really like you and I missed your nonsensical rambling". And with that he kissed me. I was so confused and so happy to be doing this again.

After what was not long enough a time, he stopped. "So you're not dumping me?", I asked.

"No" he smiled.

"Oh" I smiled.

"Okay, can I tell you now?"

"No," and I grabbed him for another kiss.

After a nice long kiss, I let go and let him come up for air. He stopped but kept my face close to his. He smiled and kissed me gingerly on the forehead, then on the tip of my nose and then my mouth and pulled back again. "Now can I tell you?", I laughed and nodded in response, making sure not to interrupt him again, he seemed determined to tell me this time.

"How much do you remember about what happened? I'd like to fill in the gaps, because I'm sure there are things that you missed that I can help with". He said it matter of fact, not with any hint of a "you're crazy let me help vibe".

"Well, I remember the pain, it was so terrible, like nothing I'd ever felt before, almost like my soul was being ripped apart." I stopped to gauge whether or not he was judging me, he seemed to be listening intently, he reached for my hand and squeezed it to encourage me to continue, "I remember I was yelling something, I heard voices and they were so sad, the feeling that came from them was pure anguish, I can't even tell you how horrible it was. I remember that I got sick and puked, I think it was from the pain. It was kind of a blur. I'm embarrassed. I don't know what happened".

"Well, I think I do. There was a lot going on. You just seemed to drop to the ground and I could tell you were in pain, you were holding your stomach and crying and saying things like "they're taking her baby, the baby, no don't take my baby, why, where is my baby?", he took a deep breath with an almost imperceptible shake of his head he continued, "it was scary, I didn't know what was happening and I couldn't understand what you were talking about. I left you on the ground for a moment to take off my shirt so I could help clean you up and I noticed something strange. We were on a bridge and down below us, there was commotion, in the water, something was happening. We were overlooking a dolphinarium, you know, one of those swim-with-the-dolphins-things."

I gasped, "I didn't know, I didn't know".

"I know that," he said and squeezed my hand again, "but somehow you knew the pain they were experiencing. The dolphins, they were, I don't know, screaming in a way, I've never seen anything like it. I saw them, they looked all riled up and there were men with nets but I couldn't leave you there, writhing on the floor, so I cleaned you up and tried to hold you until it stopped. I called your Dad and said you got really sick and that I was bringing you home".

"Did you tell my Dad about the dolphins?"

"No, I didn't know it was relevant, but I wouldn't have told him anyway, that's your story to share, not mine".

"Please don't tell anyone".

"Of course not, well, Alexa knows parts of it, but nothing about you. I needed her, for the plan."

"What plan?"

"We are going to release those dolphins back into the wild".

"What? I mean I'm in, but what?"

"I've done a lot of research, watched documentaries, and tried to learn as much as I can. It started with me going back to the bridge. That's when I realized what had happened. I overheard some people talking as they were leaving. They were saying that it was too bad the baby wasn't there anymore, but that they'd had fun anyway. It made me sick. It made sense then. You were somehow feeling what was happening. Somehow they were reaching out to you and telling you what was happening. I don't understand how that happens exactly, but I don't think that's what matters. What matters is that whales and dolphins don't belong in captivity and I have a plan to help release them and a secret campaign to help close the other dolphinariums in the area. We can start here and hopefully the rest of the world will follow".

"So you haven't called me because you were working on this?".

"Yes, I even went and paid to swim with the dolphins, even though it made me feel like crying, I pretended to love it. Alexa and I went, just to gather information and she put on a show so that I could look around without anyone noticing. Alexa was all in, she made me watch The Cove and Blackfish and she knows a lot about this apparently, she talked my ear off. She is going to help us, but we shouldn't tell anyone else."

After he outlined his plan, we decided to pack up my stuff and go up to the hotel and eat. I introduced him to my Aunt Danni and I could tell she liked him, who wouldn't? We ordered the same thing and I raised an eyebrow when he ordered. "I'm a vegetarian now," he said with a happy smile. I gave him my heart that day.

Chapter 13
My Birthday

I saw Emilio pretty much every day. Either we got together with friends, went to the beach, or just watched movies at my house. I couldn't get enough. I wanted him around all the time, but I let him take the lead, just in case, I didn't want him to get sick of me. We talked about how we would have to be apart when he went back to school in San Diego, so we wanted to spend as much time together as possible when he was here. We knew each other's families and made sure we spent time with them as well, together of course, but the more we included them, the more they trusted us and let us be alone together and as long as we spent enough time with them, they didn't question the fact that we were glued to each other.

It was July and my birthday was coming up, the 15th to be exact, and I didn't really know what I wanted to do. I definitely wasn't going to have a sweet sixteen, but I wanted to celebrate my new life. It was the first birthday I'd be without my Mom. My Mom always used to make us a crazy cake and there was always some adventure planned and it was always a surprise. One year, I think it was when I turned 10, she woke me up at midnight, with a disco ball and a 30-minute dance party. She MADE me dance and it was just her and I, dancing like fools and after half an hour, she got in my bed with me and we went to sleep, giggling and happy. Then in the morning I awoke to a packed car and a spur of the moment camping trip to Big Sur, my favorite, but we had to have the cake for breakfast because she didn't want to take it with us in the car.

I tried hard not to think about my Mom. It made me so sad and so mad at the same time. My mother abandoned us and not only that, she is crazy and has likely passed on the crazy to me. From what I read, it's in the later teenage years that you start to experience schizophrenia and in women, there is an increase in symptoms after thirty. So, I figured that when my parents married, it wasn't so bad, maybe it was mild, like what I'm experiencing and then around thirty she started to get worse. I decided to put her away in that little box in the back of my brain and not think about her now. That little box sure was getting full!

My Dad came into my room one morning, about a week before my birthday, all excited and feeling proud of himself, "I have the perfect birthday plan for you, but I want it to be a surprise." Let's put together a guest list", he sat on my bed.

"Ok", I didn't know what to say. My steady, predictable Dad seemed to be trying so many new things and approaching life with new vigor.

"I'm assuming number one on the list will be Emilio", I nodded. "I'm going to invite myself, the boys, and your Aunt Danni, but I think you would have put us on the list anyway, we can't have more than twelve, who else would you like to invite?"

"Can we invite Ruby and Alexa and maybe Theo too? I'd rather not have too many people."

"I think that's perfect. Just tell them to meet here at the house at 6:00 am and they'll need swimsuits, sunscreen and a towel, maybe a change of clothes. Basic beach gear. I know it's early, but tell them it will be worth it." He kissed me on the cheek, still excited and left.

That morning came and I bounced out of bed. This is not normal, I would never bounce out of bed at that hour, but I was excited. I got to be with my Golden God on my birthday and who knows what my Dad had in mind. I figured he found a new beach and was going to take all the gear out there for a beach party. I had packed my beach bag the night before and decided on an active swimsuit with a sundress over it, that way I could throw on a rash guard if needed, I liked using rash guards to protect me from the sun, instead of having to slather on tons of sunscreen. I grabbed my bag and headed downstairs. Aunt Danni was already there, eating breakfast which Elena was serving. Somehow, I don't think it's a Mexican thing, Elena had made eggs benedict, my favorite, I have a feeling my aunt helped with that. There were blueberry pancakes too, which I loved. In fact, I looked around and the spread was amazing, with a huge bowl of a variety of fruit, muffins, waffles, two different types of local honey and real maple syrup. People started arriving and were quickly made to sit down and eat.

I knew exactly when Emilio arrived because my heart started racing, why did he have such a strong effect on me? Not to mention Bilbo bolted to the door and started jumping at his feet. He kissed me on the cheek and hugged me, "Happy birthday Lily Louise," he lingered a moment in the crook of my neck, seemingly taking in my scent, and then he kissed my other cheek. "I got you a little gift, but I think it would be better to open it after."

"After what?"

He laughed, "I'm pretty sure your Dad said it was a surprise, so I'll let him tell you". I punched him in the arm playfully and he pretended it hurt, but laughed and grabbed my hand so I wouldn't punch him again, and just so he could hold it, I hoped.

I greeted Alexa, who handed me a gift and Ruby, who ran in and hugged me, super excited. "I almost invited Fernando", she whispered, "we're official now", but she informed me that she didn't want to intrude on my party and have someone I don't know there, which I really did appreciate. I found out that Theo had some friends in town and they went camping and surfing on the Pacific side and wouldn't be back until next week.

My Dad didn't sit down to breakfast with us, instead he was out packing up the car and who knows what, but he came in abruptly, "Okay, finish up and let's get the show on the road", he beamed. Whatever his plan was, he was more excited than any of us I think. Ollie and Luca were practically bouncing off the walls, generating their own electricity, infecting us with their enthusiasm.

We headed out to the car, but there was a huge van parked in front. Dad had rented a 12-person van so that we could all go in one car and it had plenty of room for our stuff too. Ruby handed him her phone, she had a playlist all ready to go. I had to admit I was having fun already, even though I didn't really like surprises. We waved Elena and Bilbo good bye and headed out.

It was about a two-hour road trip. I thought maybe we would sleep as it was so early, but we didn't. Everyone was talking, laughing, singing, and the energy was so happy. We arrived at a beach near La Paz.

"Okay, this is where we catch our boat, grab your stuff and head to that stand over there."

At the stand, we met our guide and boat captain. They fitted us all for masks, snorkels and fins. I'd brought mine, so I waited for the others at the shore. I was amazed at the beautiful crystal clear, aquamarine waters, they never got old, I marveled at the beauty of Baja every day.

It wasn't a yacht, it was just a simple boat, meant for no more than 12-15 people, with seating and shade over the top. My Dad explained we were going on a tour of one of the islands off shore and pointed to it in the distance. It's uninhabited and it's a protected marine reserve. Our guide, Boa, was a stocky, dark skinned Mexican with a warm smile and a fun personality. He spoke English, Italian, French and of course Spanish and he was a natural waterman who knew the area like the back of his hand. He spoke to us mainly in Spanish, which was good practice for me and I understood pretty well. When Emilio asked him something in Spanish, perfect Spanish, I almost fell out of the boat. Why didn't I know he spoke perfect Spanish? He never ceased to amaze me.

We were told that there was the potential to see tons of wildlife, that it was abundant and there were frequent sightings of whales like fin whales, minke whales and even orcas, (it wasn't whale season yet, when apparently, the waters are full of gray whales, right whales, blue whales, sperm and humpback whales-the winter months January-March).

Everywhere you turned you could see some spectacle or another. Massive frigate birds flying above, looking like their dinosaur predecessors, rays gliding along the bottom as though they too were flying. Wild fig trees clinging to the cliffs growing in seemingly impossibly configurations, faces and figures the water had carved into the rocks, blue footed boobies and so much more.

Riding along in the panga, the type of boat commonly used here in Baja, we bounced along happily pointing out whatever we saw, with Boa pointing to special points of interest and telling us stories about different things he's seen. We traveled off the coast of the island for a bit, heading towards a spot where you can snorkel with sea lions, when I got a feeling, a weird, amazing feeling, like my whole body was buzzing, a lot like when I was nearing the baby sea turtles and I suddenly knew what it was. I jumped up and grabbed my camera and yelled at the captain to stop the boat, he started to slow to a stop but before he did I had already leapt out of the boat, diving into the water.

In the excitement, I'd forgotten my mask so I couldn't see very well under the water, but I could feel, it was almost like seeing. Hundreds of dolphins of varying size began circling around me. Nudging me playfully, petting me with their heads, swimming along underneath my hands so I'd touch them. It was a nursery, with so many dolphins I was overwhelmed, but the feeling was amazing, it was so amazing that I didn't stop to worry about the fact that I heard voices. I didn't care if the voices were really theirs or if they were just in my head. Today I was carefree, I was ecstatic. They whispered my name as they swam by me, the babies wanted to play and take me to their special spots. An older dolphin neared and told me to breathe and gave me a push up towards the surface and the little ones tickled my feet, I almost choked as I surfaced, laughing.

Everyone on the boat was looking over the side, trying to understand what was happening, some yelling frantically. My Dad and Emilio had jumped in to help me I guess and were swimming towards me. "I'm okay, look, look", as I tried to point all around me while laughing hysterically. Just then they started jumping and playing around me, showing off for my friends (that's what the little ones were saying anyway.

I swam back to the boat and I told the captain which direction to go and the dolphins followed, playing in our wake, to the delight of everyone on the boat. Boa said they could be very playful, but he'd never seen them like that and he'd never seen anyone swim with them before.

We saw fin whales that day, though I restrained myself and didn't jump in, but secretly sent them warm greetings and thanked them for coming near the boat. We snorkeled at a coral reef, tucked away secretly near a sea lion colony. The sea lions had many pups and the male sea lion was protecting his territory, I warned everyone not to get too close to him and I told him we meant no harm, I don't think he cared, he was a very large and intimidating, grumpy male.

We stopped for lunch on a white sand beach where we had lunch and swam and explored. It was a glorious day and such a wonderful surprise. It would be hard to top this birthday; I would always remember my sixteenth. I'd even forgotten that it was the first birthday without my Mom.

On the ride home, I sat with Emilio and he gave me my present.

"This is the first part, the second part is at your house, I hope you like it". It was a little box and I opened it to find a sweet little dolphin necklace. It was a thin, long, delicate gold chain, with a pendant, two dolphins, facing each other, with their "foreheads" together, forming a heart. It was so sweet, and though it could border on being too cheesy, it actually had special meaning for us and it would give me the courage to carry out our plan in a few weeks.

"I love it", I said, resting my head on his chest, "I really love it, thank you". And then, he said it.

"I love YOU, Lily Louise". I couldn't be happier. A tear rolled down my face.

I didn't say it back. I was dumbstruck, again. I was overjoyed but I was also in a car with a bunch of other people and I didn't want to cause a scene or have everyone see me cry. I just stayed where I was in the comfort of his arms with my head on his chest until we got home.

As everyone was leaving, I thanked them profusely and hugged everyone and stayed on the doorstep waving everyone off. Emilio was the last to leave. I wrapped my arms around his neck and kissed him, trying to tell him how I felt with my kiss. When I pulled away, I ran my fingers through his hair while I inspected his beautiful face and he smiled.

"Well…?" he asked.

I smiled, "Well what?"

I knew what he wanted, he wanted the words, but I wanted to tease him a bit more.

"You know what" he said, feigning a frown.

"Ohhhh, good night," I said brightly, teasing him again, adding another kiss and then I pulled away turning to go inside. He grabbed my arm and pulled me back. "I worship the very ground you walk on my Golden God," I said mockingly. He stood there, not smiling or laughing. I'd gone too far. He turned to go to his car.

Wait, wait, I ran to catch him. "I love you, I love you, I love you." Then he turned and gave me that reassuring, all consuming Golden God smile of his and gave me one last kiss.

When I got to my room, there was a framed photograph on the wall. It fit right in, as if it had always been there. It was a picture of the Goat Gandalf, at least that's what we called our favorite sculpture at the marina. It was a beautiful photograph, the sculpture was back lit with the pink and orange hues of sunset, and it was blown up and framed professionally, and when I looked closely at it, I could tell it was a photo I had taken. In the corner, scrawled in small, fine print, it had the date and said,

"The day I fell in love" with a little red heart drawn next to it.

I called the girls and showed them my gifts and told them all about the day. They were so happy for me. They told me everything they'd been doing and we caught up. I missed them so much. I didn't want to think about the day that Emilio would have to go back, but I decided not to waste my time thinking about that now. Instead, I thought of "the plan" and the mission that awaited us.

Chapter 14
Operation Freedom

We had been refining the plan and trying to make it as simple as possible and we were a bit stuck. Emilio and I couldn't figure out exactly how to distract the guard. Emilio, with some help from Alexa, had done quite a bit of reconnaissance work, observing and recording guards, when they work, when they switch, the layout of the dolphinarium and the marina. It was impressive and sophisticated work for a seventeen-year-old.

We had chosen a date, next Thursday, because Thursday nights there is only one "guard" and he's young and friendly. I actually feel bad, because if we succeed, he will likely get fired, but the truth is, that this is more important and I hope because he's young that there will be many more opportunities for employment. We will try to make it look as "accidental" as possible. We were having trouble with how to lead the dolphins out of the marina, through the jetties and out into open water. I could lead them out, but it's a long swim and we need them to swim at their speed, not mine, so we needed a boat and a fourth person, but it had to be the right person.

My cousin Catarina arrived just in time. Though we'd never met before now (we'd met a few times before the age of three, but we don't remember), our chemistry and bond was instant. She was the older sister I never had and I was the sibling she never had. She was athletic, a tennis player, but all around coordinated and a good swimmer too, but more than that she is very smart and beautiful too, with her dark hair, pale skin speckled with freckles, and a broad smile. She is also a local and knows a lot of people and the area. So of course we decided to fill her in on the plan and see if she'd help.

"I know that place, it's really sad, of course I'll help".

"I realize that this is short notice and that you might be recognized, but I also think no one would suspect you either and you are smart enough to improvise if something doesn't go as planned."

"Cuzzy, now that we're together, nothing can stop us."

So now that we had our fourth, we just needed a small, quiet boat.

Emilio said we should just rent one, rent it for a couple of days, fill it with fishing gear and store it at Las Olas, but we scrapped that idea because it would be too hard to store at Las Olas, the shore was steep and the shore break there could knock you out it was so strong.

Once we filled Catarina in, she helped us refine the plan. She knew someone that worked there and would engage the guard that way, Alexa would then interrupt their conversation with her "lost" dog, played by Bilbo, who hopefully would remember my directions. He understood me very well and followed my directions, but like most dogs, his memory wasn't the best and I couldn't give him too many commands at once or he'd do the first couple and forget the rest, so I had to figure out how best to prep him for this. Luckily we play a lot of games together, like hide and seek, where I hide a treat or a toy and he has to find it. Usually he finds it super-fast, maybe because I'm picturing the hiding place.

The day had come and I felt ready. We met in the afternoon to prep. We rented a boat from the Hilton, well, Catarina did, and we filled it with fishing gear, in case anyone came close. We had double checked tides and we'd gone over the plan many times. Everyone would have a cell phone, me too, but I wouldn't really be able to use it as I'd be in the water for most of the plan.

We packed the car, Catarina's, and headed toward the marina. Alexa and I wore identical dresses and put our hair up in the same way, so it would seem there were only two people at the marina, Alexa and Catarina, and Bilbo of course. Emilio should be there already, with the boat and the gear I would need.

We arrived at sunset and Catarina, Bilbo and I got out of the car. Alexa would stay hidden in the car until she got her text to join Catarina, as me, or the girl in the flowery dress with the dog. Catarina and I walked around looking at sculptures, checking out the boats, making time for the sun to go down, we needed twilight and then darkness for our plan. The tide was coming up and the moon was new, so we wouldn't have to worry about the moonlight. We neared the boats and the marina and found the sheltered spot we'd picked out where no one could see us. I ducked down and took off my dress (I had a swimsuit underneath). Catarina stuffed my dress in her purse and handed me the black swim cap. I tucked my hair up underneath and took the goggles she held out. She smiled at me and with a wink and left to meet Alexa, I could see her texting as I slipped into the water. Before I swam away, I told Bilbo to play hide and seek, I pictured the sculpture furthest from here where I'd hidden the treat and told him to find the treat and then I hoped he'd stay. I left several hidden in the same area, hoping he'd sniff them all out and be preoccupied for enough of the time.

I swam as quietly as possible to where I knew Emilio would be waiting. He didn't look like himself and I almost laughed out loud when I saw him. He looked like a tourist and his hair was hidden up under an old baseball cap and he looked so serious.

"You okay?", I nodded, "Okay, I want you to be safe. If anything goes wrong, just get out of there and signal me to pick you up, we can always come up with another plan, be safe. With that said, I know you can do this, I wish it was me, but it has to be you, only you can talk to them."

I motioned for him to be quiet and smiled. He gave me the backpack with the wire cutters, bolt cutters and a couple of rusty locks that we made look like they just fell apart with age and rust. I started swimming towards the dolphinarium, but stayed hidden until it was dark. At this point, Catarina would be chatting up the guard and any minute now, Alexa would come running, saying her dog was lost and crying. We were hoping this would be enough to distract the guard and he would leave his post for a few minutes to help the pretty girls with the lost dog. It seemed silly, but Catarina was very smart and she would find a way to make it happen and Alexa was an aspiring actress, so I had to trust them. When it darkened enough and I had to just kind of guess at this point, I hoped they'd be on time, I just had to go for it.

I swam up as close as I could and tried to listen for voices, but I couldn't hear anything, until I heard them. There was only one way in and out of the dolphin pools, so there was only one gate to break open for them, then, I would have to get them to trust me and follow me out.

I heard, in a voice, in my head, "We knew you'd come, we knew, we've been waiting".

Is the keeper there?" I asked, don't ask me how I asked, but I asked? I heard, "He's gone".

I swam right up to the gate and started to look at the lock. They had changed the lock; it wasn't a big chain with padlocks anymore. There were some wires and a type of bike lock, the ones that use a cable, it almost looked like a surfboard leash. Which gave me an idea…

I asked one of the dolphins to go watch and make sure no people came, he was my look out, a young male dolphin. The two females stayed with me and I asked one of them to gnaw on the cable, once it got down to the wire part of it, I easily cut it with the wire cutters. I tried to jiggle the gate, to widen it until the dolphins would fit, I also tried to dent the gate so it would look like the dolphins had gnawed at the lock and pushed at the gate until they could squeeze through. I held the gate open, it was hard, but I could hold it just enough to let them through, once all three dolphins were out, I waited for the fourth. But she didn't come, I couldn't see her, but I could hear her. It was a pregnant female and she was pleading not to be left behind. I told her to come but she couldn't explain why she couldn't or I wasn't understanding. It was confusing, like she was speaking a different language where I could pick up every other word. The dolphins started speaking in their clicks and whistles but I tried to get them to be quiet. I squeezed through the gate into the pen and noticed another pen on the far side, near the bridge where I'd gone down on my BIG date. How could I forget the small pen? She was isolated and afraid and I tried to reassure her and keep her quiet. Someone was walking on the bridge. I ducked into a corner and tried to keep out of sight. I went underwater and held my breath as long as I could. I popped back up, just enough to breathe and tried to look around. The couple that was walking on the bridge had moved along but were not yet out of sight. I quietly inspected the gate to the pen and it wasn't locked, it just had a tricky latch. I had to wait until the couple was out of sight, but I then swung it open. I let her out and she swam towards the other gate, not waiting for me. I didn't know how to make this look so I just closed it and latched it again, maybe they'd think she jumped over?

I got back to the main gate and pried it open again for the pregnant female, she needed a bit more care and a bit more room. The other dolphins were waiting, which was a shock to me, they could have swum away happily, but I understood then that they didn't know where to go and they were waiting for me. I started to swim out into the marina when I realized I'd forgotten the backpack. CRAP. I had to go back, I stuck close to the docks and tried to stay underneath the boats out of view. I had dropped the backpack and it had sunk to the bottom, with the tools. It was dark and I couldn't see it. I dove to try and find it, several times, but I just couldn't see it. I looked at my watch, it was getting late, I needed to go, but I just didn't want to leave any evidence there, even underwater. As I started to take a deep inhale to dive down again, the playful little male dolphin, popped up with the backpack, he slid one of the straps over his nose. I almost screamed, he surprised me and then I was so happy I almost forgot I was in a hurry.

I slid it on my back and heard voices, Catarina was one of them. I had to go, faster, but I was tired and swimming with a heavy backpack. I swam and swam, I knew it would be a long swim, but since I was trying to swim quickly, it was that much more exhausting. I had to stop and rest, clinging to one of the docks, risking detection. I could probably be quiet enough to stay and rest for a while, but not with four dolphins, clicking and swimming and breathing. I wanted to cry, I couldn't let them down now, we were so close, I let go of the piling and started to swim again, but I was so slow.

"I've got you," I heard. One of the females slid her dorsal fin under my hand, slowing for me to hold on. She pulled me along, just under the surface, letting me up frequently for air.

It was so much faster; they were so lithe and so powerful and I felt safe with them around me. I begged them to keep quiet, to keep to the dark water, away from lights. The female continued to pull me through the water, but I felt the others disperse, it made me nervous. Then I heard it too, there was a boat coming in, a small boat, but not our boat. I told them to come close to me and stay still and when I signaled, we dove deep and swam towards the open ocean. My lungs were begging for air, but I had to stay under, just a little bit longer. When we finally surfaced, I gasped for air, had we been in the marina I would have alerted every person in a five-mile radius, but we were at the end of the jetty and the waves hitting the jetty covered my noise. I looked around and there was nothing. No boats, no people, no Emilio. I waited at the spot we were supposed to meet, it would have been creepy, just floating in the dark, in the ocean, except for the dolphins, but time was ticking. Suddenly I saw a light, the lantern, on the boat! It quietly crept around the jetty toward me and I swam towards it, the dolphins followed, cautiously. Emilio held out a hand and pulled me in.

"I'm so sorry," he whispered, "I'm so glad you're okay, I needed to hide from that boat, I'm so sorry".

"I'm okay, just a bit tired, we gotta go, but let me say good bye". I peered over the edge of the boat and put my hands in the water. The young male and the pregnant female came right up, the others on the other side where Emilio put his hands out and got a special thank you from them. I "told" them they should join the pod. I told them where I'd seen it, I couldn't explain it in words, it's not like they understand "east or west", so I pictured the way there and the island and anything else I could think of to help them find the pod, I knew they'd fit there and it would be wonderful for that baby to be born at the nursery. They sent me feelings of gratitude and joy and love.

Emilio looked to me for the okay and we made our way back toward the Hilton. We rode in silence. I think the adrenaline had our minds racing but the fact that we had succeeded in freeing those beautiful beings made us incredibly happy and satiated. We made it to the Hilton, but stayed out in the water, just floating, staring at each other, grinning from ear to ear.

"We did it," we both whispered. I started to laugh, quietly, realizing I still had that ugly swim cap on. I took it off and shoved it in the backpack which we tucked under the seat. Emilio pulled out a t-shirt and shorts and helped me put them on over my suit, without tipping the boat over. We kissed and waited and kissed some more, until we noticed Bilbo running around on the beach and Catarina waving us in.

We pulled the boat in and sat on the beach for a while. We each told what had happened and it seemed that for the most part everyone had some sort of hitch, but everyone was able to think on their feet and make it work. Catarina laughed, the guard was a friend of hers from town and he hated his job, he felt sorry for the dolphins, but still, Catarina played it cool and when Alexa came running with her lost dog story, he chivalrously came to their aid. Catarina had also noticed the isolated dolphin in the far pen and knew I would need more time, so she purposely led him away from where Bilbo would be. Alexa also purposely fell and scraped her knee, "For the cause," she said and he helped her to their car and helped clean her up, luckily there was a first aid kit in the car so he didn't have to go back to the dolphinarium to get one. All in all, it was not as long as it felt, but we were all exhausted. We all took a dip in the pool, so people would see we were there and assume we'd been there all day. Operation Freedom was a total success.

Chapter 15
Autumn

August was nearing its end and I was so busy making plans, I almost forgot to have fun. It was so hot and I had a hard time thinking clearly sometimes, but every day, Emilio and I would go to the beach around sunset. Sometimes we took the kayak out with Bilbo. Sometimes we'd take the boys to the pool at the Hilton, sometimes we hung out with Catarina and her friends, and sometimes it was just us, but every day we were together, enjoying the time we had before our inevitable separation.

We planned and planned and planned. Emilio would be heading back to start his senior year and I would be here, completing my junior and senior years in one year so that I could apply to universities with Emilio. Luckily I had taken extra credits both my 9th and 10th grade years, hoping I could have an easy senior year, so it was totally possible, and my father had found a school here where it could be done. I figured it would be great to keep super busy so I wouldn't miss him so much. We planned on which universities we'd be applying to and how we would video chat and do our college applications together, we'd go where we both got accepted, to be determined… He would come out for every holiday and school break, which his family did anyway. Since I wouldn't be playing sports, I'd have to replace that with some other extra-curricular activities, so I would be volunteering with the non-profit my Dad was working with, I would be working with their offices here and with the sea turtle nesting project. Emilio would be completing his community service hours, required for graduation at the Wild Coast San Diego office, where the girls and I used to help out.

Emilio and his family and Catarina all left the same day, it was incredibly difficult and I didn't want any sad goodbyes at the airport. One of my talents is denial, so I just pretended it wasn't happening. There was a break in November, for Thanksgiving, when I would see Emilio again, so we didn't say goodbye and I didn't cry and I was determined to focus on all that I had to look forward to.

The girls arrived two days later for Labor Day weekend and I felt like I was home. It was wonderful to see them and be with them and catch up. We hit the beach and I showed them my favorite spots. I took Eva and Sophie to all the best surf spots, the ones I knew at least, there were a lot I still wanted to explore, known only by locals who are unwilling to share. I took them to one of my favorite spots on the East Cape, just us, no Bilbo, no other friends, just the four of us.

"So your Dad is okay with you graduating early and going off to college with Emilio?" Sophie asked.

"You'd be surprised I said, he's so different, so much more relaxed, and he trusts me. I think he feels really bad that I don't have a Mom to talk to about boyfriends and stuff, so as long as I'm happy and safe, he's fine with what I want."

"My Dad would flip out," Evi said, surprisingly, as she rarely comments.

Summer took this opportunity to ask her a question, "What's going on with you and the hottie coach?"

Eva glared at Summer, "As you well know Summi, nothing is going on".

"Why not?" she pushed.

"I'm focused on the national team, I can only play this season and next and I'm sure I won't play much this season, and you know I need to do well to get a scholarship", Eva was annoyed.

Summer didn't care, she continued, "I know all of this Evi, I just want you to be happy and I think you really like him".

"We do like each other; we've talked about it." I think all our jaws hit the floor.

"Why haven't you told us?", Sophie screeched, "We tell you everything!"

"Because we decided not to do anything about it. He's older and I have a lot to do if I want to make the national team and play in a world cup someday."

"If it's meant to be, it's meant to be."

"See, she gets it, thank you Lily." Eva shot me a look that said thank you.

"Well, I meant that just because the timing isn't perfect, it doesn't mean it won't work out, you can make it work if…",

I stopped, I was comparing my own situation and it wasn't the same, "no, I did mean if it's meant to be, it'll happen, whether it's now or later."

"What about Blake?", Sophie changed the subject, putting the attention back on Summi.

"Well, we are kind of on and off, right now off, I met this other guy, Will, he's hot and works at the skate shop, and he's a senior, wants to be a lawyer, unusual I know, right now we are just doing homework together, but I'm making the situation work to my benefit, I know he likes me, so stay tuned."

Sophie was still with Chris and since we'd known him since elementary school, there wasn't much to ask, we loved them together, it was a sweet relationship and we saw Prom King and Queen in their future.

They were bummed not to have met Emilio, but they would meet him in San Diego, working at Wild Coast, so that would be good enough.

Eva looked like she had something to say, but couldn't quite bring it up. "What is it?", I asked.

Sophie spoke instead, "I think I know," she looked at Eva who nodded, "she, well, we don't understand why you won't talk about certain…things."

"Things?"

"Yes, things, like the incident, and your Mom. I mean we know you, you are brave and strong, but you are also stubborn and…"

There was a very long silence while I debated. I didn't think they would ever confront me about any of this. Maybe they know. I mean, they really, really know me, they must be noticing that I'm changing and that I need to face facts.

"Well," I finally spoke, it was hard to find my voice, "when my Mom left, I found out that she's, well, crazy, or mentally ill, or whatever the appropriate words are, let's just say crazy. I don't know exactly what her illness is because she left and didn't stop to mention it before leaving, but I think from the pills I found that maybe she was, I mean is, schizophrenic, and I've read a little about it and it seems, with all the weird things that happen to me, that maybe I have it too, I think

I'm crazy and I am living in denial, trying to just be happy, with all these changes, and…"

"Wait, whoa" Eva cut me off. She looked at me like she didn't know what to say and then looked at the other girls.

"You know that people who think they are crazy are not actually crazy right?" Summer said confidently.

"Yeah, everyone knows that," Sophie chimed in, "don't you think we'd tell you if you were? I mean, we're nice, but we're not that nice," she winked at me and we laughed.

"But I hear voices sometimes" I couldn't believe I'd just said it, out loud.

"Well I don't know anything about that, or what you hear, or what goes on in your head," Summer stated, with the voice of an expert, "we've known you most of your life and I've seen weird things happen to you but none of it tells me that you are crazy. I may not be an expert in mental illness, but I know you are nothing like your Mom. You never knew anything different, but we all knew your Mom was different, the longer you knew her, the more evident it was. We just don't see that with you, it's something else."

Sophie reassured me in her own way, "Yeah, I mean you ramble like a crazy person sometimes, but that's a personality quirk, not a mental illness" the other girls started laughing.

"Evi never talks, she's definitely crazy, so you're not alone" Summi joked.

Evi glared at her and then smiled.

"I guess we all have our issues."

"What I want to talk about is the incident, Summer said. "What happened, I mean, I think that I know, at least I know what I saw."

"It has happened again." I proceeded to tell them about what really happened on the BIG date and about Operation Freedom and the dogs and the birds and anything I could think of and I rambled, but they listened without interruption or question. "So that's it, what do you think?"

"We always knew something was up with you, but you never wanted to talk about it, and anytime we'd try, you'd shut down, so we left it alone," this coming from Eva, the ultimate non-talker.

"You can always talk to us, we will never think you are crazy, unless of course a real doctor proves it to us, but we know you're not. But, for fun, let's call your special little talent, your "crazy" or "the crazy" it can be our code," Summer suggested.

"Yes, it will be like laughing at it and it won't be so scary, maybe you can learn to embrace it someday and use it somehow, like you already have." Sophie hugged me and squeezed my shoulders, her way of telling me I was fine.

The next day, I took the girls to the airport. I didn't want to, no goodbyes, just hugs and see you laters. But now everyone was gone, my Golden God, my cousin and my best friends. I would just have to dig in, stay busy and wait for my people to come back to me.

I got home and Dad was at the table with the boys. "Ready for school tomorrow?"

"I guess so. I like that the boys will be at the same school, though I'm sure it's going to be way different than Mar Vista High."

"It's a lot smaller, but you are doing so well here Sweets, you'll be fine and you can drive the boys, after they adjust."

School was fine, nothing exciting or special. It was pretty great walking the boys to their class, they were so excited and of course made instant friends. As I walked to my first class I saw Ruby standing by the door. She ran up to me, "I convinced my Dad to let me switch," she grabbed my hand and led me in and we sat next to each other. "He was resistant at first but once I explained you were coming here and that we could be study buddies, he agreed."

"I'm really glad you are here Ruby."
"Ditto."

We had some classes together, but since I had to pack a couple extra classes in, I would be staying later in the day and I had a different lunch time. It was a small private school, very small, but it had the most amazing courtyard and greenhouse. I kept to myself and really only knew Ruby, her boyfriend Fernando, and his friend Santiago, Santi for short. Because I didn't have lunchtime or break with Ruby, I found a quiet, cool spot in the Greenhouse, where I could be alone, read, and enjoy a little quiet time to myself. Ruby says I'm just hiding from the world, maybe I am. I feel vulnerable out there, it's hard to explain, but I know I don't feel that way when HE is here.

I studied hard and went to the beach often, and every night I had a video call from Emilio. I felt like I was adjusting and before I knew it, the end of October neared and the weather started to cool, it was actually the most amazing warm weather (no longer scorching), calm seas, and warm water. I was counting the minutes for Thanksgiving when he would be here again.

Chapter 16
The Organic Market and Frida

With November came warm waters, perfect weather, and the Mercado Organico. The Organic Market is every Saturday and it's a regular outing for the family. My Dad helps them out a bit, he's on the board, so he has to be there early, but the boys and I always go about mid-morning and my Aunt meets us there as well. It's just a wonderful atmosphere, with a hundred booths or so that sell everything from organic produce/food to art and jewelry made by local artisans. There are live bands each week and a unique crowd of Mexican bohemians, ex pats, and kids of all ages running around.

Each week we'd get there and the boys would immediately take off, reappearing when hungry or thirsty. I'd have my wheatgrass shot at my favorite stand and then I'd have some food under the mango tree, listening to music or watching some performance. There is definitely a crowd of regulars and you start to get to know them and the people that run the booths, it's a warm, friendly place to be.

There was this older woman I would always see, doing her grocery shopping, she was always impeccably dressed and accessorized, with interesting, usually traditional Mexican attire. She usually did her hair in two braids that she piled atop her head. She was beautiful and reminded me of Frida Kahlo, so in my head I called her Frida. I made up stories for the quirky characters that frequented the market and I took a lot of pictures.

One Saturday, I saw Frida speaking to my Aunt Danni and I had to find out who she was, I walked over as casually as I could muster, but I felt excited and I wasn't sure why. My Aunt hugged me, she was the best hugger I knew, and she always made me feel loved. She asked me about my brothers and then proceeded to introduce me to Chavela, which is a nickname for Isabel, I was secretly disappointed her name wasn't Frida, but her reaction to meeting me was a bit unexpected, so I soon forgot.

Chavela, as she insisted I call her, immediately kissed me on the cheek as is the customary greeting in Mexico, but she then grabbed me by the shoulders and looked into my eyes and then began to inspect my face and my body and then, she closed her eyes and put her forehead to mine and breathed deeply. "Yes, you are right Daniela, she is special, bring her to my house tomorrow, we need to have some tea," and with that, she was off, with her colorful bag of veggies.

"What was that about?", I asked, in wonder as I watched her walk toward the exit.

"She's a beautiful soul, you'll love her, very interesting woman, and she sees something in you."

"What do you mean, what does she see?"

"I'm not sure, just wait and see, tomorrow will be an eye-opening day for you."

The next morning, my Aunt Danni showed up and we had breakfast together. She told my Dad we were going to explore the little town of Santiago, while he and the boys went surfing on the Pacific side of the peninsula.

Santiago was about an hour or so drive east, a quaint little town, quite charming and a bit isolated, it's claim to fame being that it sits right on the Tropic of Cancer. We pulled up to her house, but there was nothing really to see in the front, except that it was a blue house, with a bright green door, I loved it and took photos of course.

The house was designed as a square with an immense courtyard in the middle. There was happy, folksy, traditional Mexican music blaring and my Aunt knew that we wouldn't be heard knocking so we just entered, after all she was expecting us.

We entered the room that basically just had doors that were open to the courtyard and the courtyard called to us. It was incredible and huge, you couldn't see the other sides there was so much greenery. Fruit trees and flowers that smelled incredible, giant birds of paradise towered over our heads, it was like entering a well-manicured jungle. It was fresh, not just cool, but the air was so fresh and so inviting. My Aunt called out and from behind a gorgeous tree with red flowers came Doña Chavela carrying a tray with tea, she set it down, greeted us warmly, and went to turn down the music.

I noticed parrots flying about the garden and tried to "hide" from them, but I knew I wouldn't be able to for very long. I sensed at least five macaws, a pair of lovebirds and a pair of cockatoos, not to mention dozens of hummingbirds. Chavela sat down and we had pleasant conversations over tea, very dignified, but not terribly life changing. After tea, she looked to my Aunt and said that she had some interesting books for her to explore and they were all laid out in the library. My Aunt knew that was her cue and left us alone.

"Little flower do you sense me?", she asked matter-of-factly.

"I, I, I don't know what you mean" I stuttered.

"I think you do, you just don't know it yet. Did you ever see me at the market before? Did you feel drawn to me?"

Risking that I might sound like a stalker, I answered honestly, "Yes, in a way, I always noticed you and felt the need to take your photo and I wanted to meet you."

"Yes, that's it, you just aren't in tune with your gift, it's growing in strength though, I can feel it and you need some help, you're struggling."

What on earth was going on here, who was this crazy lady? "I'm not sure I know what you mean."

"Don't let the logical part of your brain hold you back, stop trying to talk yourself out of what's happening and just let it happen."

She stared at me, silently, I felt like she was picking through my brain. I couldn't speak, but even if I could, I wouldn't know what to say, it was a strange sensation. After many minutes of this uncomfortable silent prodding, I let my guard down for just a moment and let my instincts take over and I called the birds to me. I closed my eyes for a second, just barely longer than a blink, and they were all there. Her pet parrots, all the ones I'd sensed. Some were perched on my chair, some on the table next to us, some in the trees, and I had two humming birds sitting on my hand and the beautiful blue hyacinth macaw on my shoulder. Chavela smiled at me and whispered, "Yes, that's it, don't hold back." We sat, still and quiet, as did the birds, awaiting further instructions, they nuzzled me and prodded me at times, but for the most part they were just still and content. "Now, let them go."

I told them to go, and basically just released them somehow, except for the blue macaw, he didn't leave. "He wants to stay for a while."

She laughed a hearty lovely, intoxicating laugh, "That's Pancho, he's a stubborn, lovable old man, tell him he can stay."

She started to ask me some uncomfortable questions, "Can you do that with all animals? Usually, from what I've encountered, there are just specific species, but I see that all the birds seem to respond to you, also do you hear them or how do you communicate?" There were so many questions I didn't know which to answer or how to answer.

"It's birds, and dolphins, and dogs I guess." She shook her head.

"No my little flower, I'm sure it's more than that, and it's very rare, very rare." She thought for a moment, with her eyes closed and then spoke again, "I have gifts too. As you might have noticed I have an especially green thumb. I don't exactly communicate with plants, but I can feel them and know what they need and I have an excellent ability to nurture and grow things. But my other gift is that of recognizing when someone else has a gift, seeing it and helping to nurture the gift as well. I felt you at the market, but I knew you would come to me eventually, I just knew somehow, someday it would happen, and it did."

I think my mouth was hanging open because she laughed again. "I'm known by certain people for my abilities, many local farmers ask me to come and take a look at their crops and figure out what they need, I'm a consultant of sorts, no one really questions my abilities. Perhaps if I lived elsewhere, people would think I'm crazy. Do I seem crazy to you? Do you believe me?"

"No, I mean yes, I mean no I don't think you are crazy, yes I believe you."

"You can sense it, can't you?"

"Yes," I let out a long-drawn-out sigh. It felt like I was releasing a huge amount of weight off my shoulders, really if I'm honest, it felt like I was releasing a heaviness that was weighing on my soul.

"Have you ever thought that you might be mentally ill? It's a frequent occurrence among the truly gifted."

"Yes, but my mother", I started to say when she put up a hand and interrupted me.

"I don't know what you are going to say next, but it's not valid. You have a gift, a strong gift, stronger than I've seen in quite a long time, maybe ever, and it's growing in power and intensity. You need to stop worrying about being crazy and start learning to control it, harness it, and use it with purpose, always for good. I will help you, but you don't really need me, you just need to listen to yourself and the animals and your answers will come. Let's practice some meditation, it will be useful for you." And the lessons began.

My Aunt Danni and I were driving home and I was quiet. I could tell she wanted to ask me about what Chavela said, but didn't dare pry.

"You were right Aunt Danni, that was life changing." She smiled at me and we drove home in peaceful silence.

That night I talked to Emilio and the girls and "came out" as an animal empath. The girls laughed and said they were still going to call it my "crazy" and of course they were full of "I told you so's". Emilio was quiet, which worried me at first, but he was only quiet because he said of course he knew I was special and that he was very glad I was learning about it, he let me talk and talk without interruption.

I would see Chavela every Saturday at the Mercado and we would practice meditation, she would guide me and it was always centered on animals, the ocean, and nature in general. She said that when the whales came, I would need to go see them, she felt that was very important. She said she also felt another strong nurturer in my life, "he's not here physically right now, but he's always with you." What a strange thing to say, but then again, Chavela often said strange, cryptic things that I didn't always understand.

Before I knew it, Thanksgiving time was here and so was Emilio. There is no Thanksgiving in Mexico, but the weather is so nice in Baja at this time, it's tourist season and the town comes to life after the scorchingly-hot, slow days of summer. It's a festive time of year in general and all the beautiful organic produce made for an excellent Thanksgiving dinner that we shared with the Baggins family, my Dad's friends, including the mysterious DJ who had come back from his summer in Seattle, and a few of the locals we worked with at Wild Coast and the sea turtle project. It was a traditional Thanksgiving dinner in an unconventional place.

That Saturday, Emilio and I went to the Mercado as I usually did, I couldn't wait for him to meet Doña Chavela. We arrived and had a wheatgrass shot and a bite to eat, we sat in my favorite spot under the mango tree and just enjoyed being together, we couldn't get enough, we had to make up for all the time we were apart. Our parents joked about us being glued to each other and how we didn't even notice the rest of the world, but we didn't care or comment.

"She's here," he said, as he nuzzled my neck.

"Hahaha, how do you know," I couldn't imagine he'd seen her with his face in my neck and hair and then she was there, standing over us, smiling.

"There you are," I stood up to hug her and apologize for not being at our meditation spot but she gently pushed me aside after our hug. "I knew I'd meet you, you're the nurturer."

Emilio jumped up to meet her but looked confused, but I'm sure I looked even more confused.

"Mucho gusto Señora, soy Emilio," he politely introduced himself in his perfect Spanish.

"Yes, it's nice to meet you, but let's forget the small talk, shall we? I sense you aren't here for much longer and we need to talk."

She took him away and told me to meditate at our spot until she arrived. I followed her orders but I was distracted by my thoughts and I just couldn't imagine what she was saying to him. I hope she didn't scare him off or say something shockingly truthful, as she did at times. When they came to meet me, they were laughing and Emilio was carrying her bag of veggies.

"I'll see you next week my little flower. I'll give you time with your nurturer. Hasta luego!" And she was off, with a wave and a smile.

"What happened, what did she say, she's my nurturer, what was she talking about?" I couldn't get out all the questions I had, my tongue wouldn't move fast enough and then I was stopped with a kiss.

"I'll save the extra details for later, but basically, she said I have a gift too." I remained quiet so he would elaborate. "She said I'm a nurturer too, but different from her, she said my gift is attached to a person, not just any person, you specifically." I didn't know what to say and I wanted him to keep talking, I just squeezed his hands, prompting him to tell me more. "She told me that I would help you with your gift, that I would keep you stable and safe and I would come to understand what you need and not let your gift overwhelm you and that I will be your protector, so you can use your gift without fear. She said that without me, it was possible, that anxiety could hold you back, make you deny your gift, kind of mess with your mind as I understood it. She also said that while you use your gift, I can keep you physically safe. She said a lot, but she made me feel so comfortable, although it was a lot to take in, I understood what she was trying to say and I think I knew it deep down, but I always just thought they were feelings that came with loving you so much. Basically, it just means we are meant to be together, always." He kissed me then and it felt almost like an out of body experience, like we were finally understanding ourselves and our connection to each other.

It was so wonderful having everyone I loved in town, it was hard to think they'd be leaving so soon. Ruby suggested we have a bonfire at one of the East Cape beaches, as a sort of "fall festival", a send-off to our loved ones who would be leaving and a promise of the winter to come, when we would see them again. It was a small group, Catarina, Emilio, Theo, Alexa, Ruby, Fernando and Santi. We kept it small and simple and had a great time listening to music, dancing under the stars, we even had a group night swim, in the warm, clear waters of the Sea of Cortez.

As we were sitting by the fire, I asked the group if they wanted to help me with an idea that had been brewing in my head. I proposed we form a small, secret society, dedicated to caring for the planet, specifically the ocean and its beings. As the youth of Cabo, it was our responsibility to conserve its beauty and life for ourselves and for future generations.

I told them I had this idea to have a very public identity for our group but to secretly have other "missions" that no one could know about. As I threw out some of my ideas, like making our public mission to reduce and hopefully eliminate the use of plastic (for now targeting plastic bags and plastic bottles), and a secret mission to close down the dolphinariums and release the dolphins being held captive.

Everyone seemed to get excited and started to brainstorm how to accomplish our goals and what we should be called. We decided that our covert name would be Sentinels of the Sea and that our public identity would be known as Guardianes de la Tierra (Guardians of the Earth). We decided to start our public identity with a booth at the Organic Market where we would give out information on the plastic problem and give away cloth/reusable grocery bags and glass or ceramic water bottles. Everyone had a lot of ideas for the booth and we gave ourselves some responsibilities and decided to meet once a week (the out-of-towners would join us via web cam). It would be difficult with all our different schedules, but if we could keep the booth running, then the covert missions could take place when everyone was in town. We decided Ruby and Fernando would be in charge of the booth. Santi would be creating all of our images/designs and take care of digital graphics and social media. The Bagginses would be sending us bags and water bottles from the states. Catarina, Emilio and I would design the covert operations (since we had successfully done it before. Alexa and Theo were soldiers, ready for orders at any time. We planned for a while longer before deciding to return to our celebrations. Emilio made me promise not to take on any missions without him, I agreed, after all, he is my protector.

This time when he left, I did drive him to the airport, actually, I drove him and his family to the airport, and I did cry. I could only look forward to Christmas time when he would be here again.

Chapter 17
The Farm

So my Dad, the brilliant, high priced, high powered lawyer, who wore Tom Ford suits with fashionable ties, every single day to work, decided to become a farmer. He says that he's still going to do his work for the foundation, but now he also wants to have a family business. He feels that it's important for us to work the land, provide organic food for people, and have a sort of family legacy that he can pass on to his children and grandchildren and whatever. If I thought before he'd lost his mind, this just proves it. My Dad went to Harvard Law School and now he's a farmer? I can't imagine he knows anything about growing organic sweet potatoes and corn. I know he loves Thanksgiving, but are we going to raise turkeys too? He laughed when I asked him that. I think I need to stop trying to figure him out. I definitely need to stop worrying about him, "Stop worrying Sweets," is what he always tells me, followed by a pinch of the cheek or a quick squeeze. I always say, "Ok Dad," but it's easier said than done.

Today I decided to go with my Dad to the farm, which he's calling Tabula Rasa Farm. He wanted it as a clean slate or a fresh start. I realize now why he's been getting home so late, the farm is somewhat far from town. After driving out of the city, you pass several very small towns, including Santiago, some towns are more like just a few houses with a little store, and then after about an hour of that you turn off onto a dirt road and basically drive until it ends. On the way there, we had to slow down for a small herd of donkeys who were hanging out in the middle of the road. I sent them an image of cars and the road and the feeling of danger, they all looked straight at me and sort of bobbed their heads and moved to the side of the road and headed in toward the bush. My Dad laughed and looked at me, "I could have sworn they were looking straight at you," I just shrugged and said nothing, trying not to draw more attention to it, and he shook his head a bit, and just kept driving.

I try really hard not to do "stuff" in front of people, especially my Dad, my brothers have noticed some, like the birds, but they don't notice much about other people, they're little and just into themselves and whatever trouble they are amusing themselves with in the moment. I worry about my Dad noticing. I'm still not sure about everything Chavela has said, this "animal empath" thing as she calls it, might still just mean I'm crazy like my Mom, but I'm starting to come around, though I try not to let my Dad see the crazy. Sometimes it's hard to restrain myself and sometimes I just can't control it anyway.

Before, when my Dad was a lawyer and we lived a "normal" life in San Diego, I didn't see my Dad very much. That sucked, he worked crazy hours and seemed super stressed all the time and when he was home, he was still working, but he didn't really notice me. I also had my Mom as a buffer, her crazy by far overshadowed mine.

The one thing I will say about the farm is that my Dad LOVES it! He truly loves being a farmer. As he walked me through the fields, talking about when he planted this and how much it's grown and what he wants to do next, I saw a side of him I really liked to see. I'm not sure what it is, a feeling of peace and fulfillment maybe? I don't know, but it's good to see him out of his suit, full of dirt, and happy.

He went to talk to one of his field hands (he only has two right now, between the two of them they are working a 15-acre farm), I wandered off and tried to stay out of the way. I decided to explore a little. It was pretty hot, but that's nothing new, good ole Baja, but there was a little breeze that made it just tolerable. I stopped by the car and grabbed my hat, a must here, especially since I burn so quickly.

Since most of the farm had been cleared for planting, there wasn't much to explore, but bordering the farm on one side is a bit of a hill and wilderness beyond. I remembered my phone in my pocket for some music, but I'd left my headphones in the car, so I would just use it to take some photos. As I reached the top of the hill, I saw exactly what I expected to see, more wild Baja. Plenty of cactus, which are pretty cool, but it was just more of the same brush and difficult stuff to walk through. You would need a machete to carve a trail, like in the movies, though it's not lush jungle, it is lush desert, if you can imagine such a thing.

 I'll admit, when I first got here, I overlooked the desert part of Baja. The ocean, right away, takes all of your attention, it's so blue and beautiful, and it's weird once you notice that the desert meets the sea and you're standing next to a cactus while gazing at the impossibly blue waters of the Gulf of California or Sea of Cortez, (I'm still not sure why it has two names). Anyway, what I was trying to say is that the desert itself is pretty cool. Nature has designed everything here to thrive in sometimes impossibly hot temperatures. Every cactus and succulent has little "roads" on it that lead straight down to its roots to make sure it captures and takes advantage of every drop of water. Everything is spiky and warns you to "back off", which ensures it won't get eaten or trampled. Everything here is made to survive. So I too just need to learn to adapt and survive, inspired by the desert.

I continued wandering and taking photos of cool stuff I found until I was tired and very hot. I stupidly forgot to bring any water so I just looked for a shady spot. I closed my eyes and felt around for any snakes, nope, I got nothing, so I had a seat on a rock under what passes for a tree here (I sure do miss the redwoods of Big Sur sometimes). As I took my hat off and started picking the stickers out of my socks, some bees start buzzing around me. How annoying! I like bees for what they do for the environment and they really seem to like me, but the buzzing can be too much. I closed my eyes and visualized some flowers I saw on my walk and they buzzed around my head once more and took off. Wow, I'm either really losing my mind or I'm embracing this "gift" because I find I don't even stop to think about what I'm doing sometimes, I just do it.

I started to look through my photos and saw that I'd gotten some pretty good ones, some new plants I hadn't seen before that I'd identify when I got home. As I reached the end of my photos, I saw that it was getting late, hopefully my Dad would be ready to go home, I wasn't really in the mood to pull weeds or till soil, and I had homework to do. Just then, my phone died. Ugh. I sure love my iPhone, but the battery is crap.

As I looked around, I saw it had happened once again. I was lost. My parents often say that my head is always "somewhere else" and that I don't pay attention to where I'm going and that I've been like that since I was little. They have told me countless stories of me getting lost at Disneyland, the grocery store, the park, even at the post office once, they found me in a mail cart, petting a mouse! So here I was again. Hot, thirsty, tired, and lost. I had been too busy taking pictures to notice where I was going. Since there is so much of the same cactus and wildlife, it kinda all looks the same. I wondered if I should stay put and let someone find me eventually or try and find my way out, potentially wandering even further from the farm, my sense of direction isn't great. To try and avoid the embarrassment of a search party wasting time on me, I decided to figure it out on my own.

I continued for what seemed like another hour or so and nothing seemed familiar, but something familiar finally popped out at me. A cactus! I know, there are too many to count around here, but this was one of the big ones, a Cardon, I think they're called. They're cool because they can grow very tall and have a lot of "arms" and birds like to perch on top. On this one, there were about seven birds, each perched at the top of an arm. They were really cool looking birds; I'd never seen them before. They are black and white with large orange beaks. They look like a cross between a falcon and a vulture (which I found out later is exactly what they are, called Caracaras) and all at once they turned to look at me. It was very intimidating, these are some big birds and I know nothing about them. I always feel more comfortable around an animal I've encountered before or at least researched. I started to move and their gazes followed my every move. Darn, they were definitely checking me out. Those birds could eat me! I was starting to get scared. I was lost and about to be eaten by birds. If they didn't eat me, they'd do some damage, maybe peck my eyes out or something. Was I invading their territory? Maybe they felt threatened by me and I didn't know if I should try out my "power". Would I be giving in to the crazy? I guess if it works and I believe it works, I might be crazy. If I didn't try, I could be pecked to death like in *Alfred Hitchcock's The Birds,* or I could continue wandering aimlessly in the desert until I died or was humiliated by rescue.

None of my options were good, but I guess being secretly crazy was the best, so I closed my eyes and reached out to the birds. Right away I got an answer from them! They were concerned for me, not hungry or trying to eat me! At least that's what I was receiving or my crazy brain thought it was receiving! Either way I was so relieved. I closed my eyes again and opened myself up to them. They sent me an image of a carcass, maybe a coyote? Either way it was red and mangled and so gross. I felt they were offering it to me, noticing before I had, that I was very hungry. I tried sending them a "no thank you" message but that's kind of hard to do, at least I haven't figured it out yet. So instead I sent them the image of the farm. There was a pause and then they seemed to all start squawking at the same time, it was loud and I knew that they weren't talking to me, but each other. They stopped and all looked at me again. Then all at once, they flew off, but not too far, to another cactus in fact and I could still see them. I got the image of the farm sent back to me and I realized that they were showing me the way. We went on like that for about an hour. They would fly off, find another spot and wait for me to catch up. At one point, they flew too far ahead and I had to follow their very unique squawks until I found them. Soon I climbed a hill and there was the farm. A sense of joy and relief hit me all at once and I wanted to send them an image of gratitude, but didn't know how, so I just tried to send the feelings. They stayed until I reached my father's side and then took off, flying in formation, swooping and diving over the farm for several minutes and then flying off. I watched them until they were no longer visible and then my Dad asked "You get lost again?", and smirked, not waiting for an answer. "I thought you were in the car reading, until about half an hour ago" he said.

"Oh, sorry", I mumbled.
"That's ok, I figured you were on your way back from wherever you wandered off to".
"Huh, how?", I looked up at him.
"The birds", was all he said and wrapped his arm around me and walked me toward the car.

I have to say that on the ride home, I worried. I worried what he observed, what he noticed, what he thought. But I didn't dare ask him to elaborate on his comment about the birds. He didn't ask me about it or bring it up again either. I worried that he was starting to notice the crazy and that maybe he was noticing things about me that reminded him of my mother. Sometimes I want to ask him, but I don't dare, because then I might find out the truth and I'm not sure I want to know.

Chapter 18
Whale Magic

Had you asked me at the end of May if I would be happy living in Cabo, the answer would have been a matter of fact, NO! But it's so strange how life and circumstances can change, I don't think I'd want to be anywhere else, in a way, I think (and this could be the crazy talking) I'm meant to be here.

Early December was a busy time, the Guardians of the Earth were busy with booth planning, we had our logos, we'd made patches and made stickers (though the stickers were part of the Sentinels and said things like, you swim with dolphins=you kill dolphins with blood stains or bloody dolphins, they were gruesome but sent a strong message, some said "How would you like to live in a bathtub for the rest of your life?", things like that). The water bottles and bags, at least the first batch were being shipped to us, we got donations from some local organizations and would have a donation box at our booth, hopefully people would donate when they took a bag or bottle. Informing the public was a huge part of this, so I researched and got info to Santi who created pamphlets (though we didn't really want to waste paper) and collected videos about plastics and the ocean (like the one about the floating island of plastic, in the Pacific Ocean, the size of Texas). We wanted maximum impact, delivered with an innocent smile so no one would suspect us of covert operations. Chavela, my Dad, and my Aunt Danni supported our efforts and spread the word about our booth, soon we had a good crowd visiting our booth every Saturday. Every once in a while, we'd hand out bags in front of the big grocery store here in San Jose, our goal was to be the first city in Mexico to completely eliminate plastic bags and bottles.

It was a great project that really unified our group and brought us closer together and I still felt connected to Emilio and Catarina while they were away, though I missed them terribly, especially my Golden God. With the Sentinels, a jam-packed school schedule, and my kayak outings with Bilbo, I didn't have time to think about the crazy or how much I missed my Mother.

My "meditation" practice with Chavela continued and sometimes she would actually let me ask questions. Of course I knew, thanks to the Karate Kid, that there was more to my meditation practice than I currently understood, I didn't want to waste a precious question on that because I assumed someday it would become clear.

"Are you sure I'm not just a crazy freak?" This was always on my mind after all.

"I'm sure", she smiled, "you have a gift and I'm here to nurture it, I've told you that, but maybe you are a freak, of nature," she winked at me.

"Haha," I said sarcastically.

"Look, you think you are a freak because you think you are the only one", she stated with her knowing confidence. "There are others with gifts as well, but you are unique, stronger than any I've seen with your gift and it's also special because you have your own nurturer/protector. I will only be able to nurture you for a time, while Emilio grows in his gift and takes over full time. I'm a nurturer, able to help most with gifts, but again, there are others. Let's walk". We walked around the Market, and she pointed out different people to me. "See there, the wheatgrass girl, she's an empath. She senses people's energy and mood and absorbs it. Because she has grown up without a nurturer, her gift will never be fully developed, she probably thinks she has an anxiety disorder or low self-esteem, and she's likely been told her whole life she's "too sensitive," but in fact, she has strong abilities and hopefully she has found ways to shield herself, it can be lonely and painful. Oh, how about the boy that works your booth."

"Fernando?"

"Yes, he has a gift as well, he's a persuader, he's the perfect person to be in your booth, he has the ability to convince even the most set in their ways. Luckily he is not overly strong, it could be dangerous and I won't nurture his gift."

"Why not? Shouldn't all gifts be nurtured?"

"Some I'm not able to nurture, some don't need to be nurtured, and others can be dangerous. If Fernando's gift were a bit stronger and he were nurtured, he could conceivably achieve mind control, which is incredibly dangerous, just think of the implications if he gained power and used it with bad intentions." She shivered at the thought. "I once met a tree talker, his name was Diego, an interesting man. People used to make fun of him because he hugged trees, he actually hugged trees, but what people didn't know was that the trees spoke to him, told him all that they had seen, how they felt and other things he wouldn't share. He works in the forests of Humboldt, fighting logging in the old growth forests and he plants trees all over the world. The trees he plants grow at 10 times the normal rate. I think he's spending some time in the Amazon now, trying to replace what they are cutting down. He's quite fascinating and his gift is so strong, but people just write him off as a tree hugging hippie. People are not always what they seem Little Flower. Your brothers, I sense a gift in them, not developed yet, but I will keep an eye on them."

I stopped asking questions, I didn't want to push my luck, she's never said this much before, it was always about the meditation.

Sooner than I could have imagined, the Holiday break had arrived and so had my people. Catarina arrived first and we spent a few days catching up and hanging out with her Mom. I was lucky she shared her Mom with me, it didn't even occur to her to be jealous or petty, she was as happy to have a sister as I was and we always laughed at things only we understood. When Emilio arrived, I felt complete again and ready for winter break.

Our first meeting of the Sentinels birthed a new plan of action. We decided to target the various kiosks in San Jose and San Lucas that offered swimming with dolphins at the various dolphinariums. We had designed a campaign that would hit all the targets within the span of 48 hours (there were many). We designed it so that no target would be hit in exactly the same way so that it couldn't be tied to any of us. We dressed as much like tourists as we could and altered our appearances in simple ways, hats, sunglasses, and even wigs. This was strictly a sticker campaign (at least this phase would be), targeting the kiosks would hopefully deter tourists from purchasing these dolphin "adventures". We hit hard and we hit quick. Alexa was especially gifted at this particular mission. She smiled her sweet smile and "accidentally" knocked her purse into the kiosk, then pulled out the stickers and put them where they wouldn't be noticed by the salesman, but definitely seen by anyone approaching the kiosk from the front. She even went as far as filling out the reservation form (with false info of course) and then pretending she forgot her Mom's credit card at the hotel. She changed her outfit and her approach each time, sometimes worked with a partner, and was always confident and successful. She hit six kiosks that day, hopefully not too many to get her noticed. Emilio and I had a different approach, we pretended to be these lovebirds that couldn't stop making out (a tough job I know) and we'd make the sales person (this worked a bit better with females) so uncomfortable, they wouldn't make eye contact and they'd leave us alone for a minute while we stickered their kiosk. I felt bad about the salespeople, I'm sure they worked on commission and we were ruining their chances of earning for a few days, but at the same time, I hope they'll read our stickers and educate themselves enough to realize they need to find a new job.

Fernando and Santi had a different approach, they'd befriend the guys and ask about what the best clubs were for picking up girls, while Ruby or Catarina snuck up at some point and placed the stickers. Ruby and Catarina had to be most careful as they had grown up here and might be recognized and Theo was the driver. He wasn't a good actor and the whole thing made him super uncomfortable, but he wanted to help and he knew his way around, so he was the perfect driver for the getaway car.

We felt good about our successes though we would never know exactly how much of an impact, if any, we made. We figured that if we deterred or changed the mind of even one person, then that was success. We decided the Sentinels would lay low and plan a new campaign for Spring Break.

Emilio and I were together every moment possible and Christmas, though it felt strange in warm weather, it was different and amazing. For a tree, we used a kyote, which is a type of cactus flower that grows tall and when the flowers begin to die, they petrify and are shaped like a Christmas tree, our desert tree. My Dad found a huge one near the farm and cut it down (the cactus remained to grow another kyote) and we put it in a large pot with dense soil and rocks and then decorated it just like a Christmas tree, it just wasn't green. As a gift, I'd had Joa, an artisan at the market who makes jewelry, make me something special for Emilio. I'd decided to have it made from the wood of a torote tree, which glistened gold in the right light. I asked for it to be made in the shape of a shield and I asked her to carve a whale tale on it. This way it would represent Baja (the torote tree), the shield was him (a protector) and the whale tale represented the ocean and its residents. I had her make it long with a twisted hemp cord, to make it manly, but I didn't expect he would wear it, I just wanted him to have it and know that I loved him and valued him and that I felt protected. He said he loved it and promised to wear it always, but I knew I'd never be as good at gift giving as he was. He got me books, which I love, I could never have enough books (they aren't so easy to come by down here) and they were all inspirational stories about people I admired like Jane Goodall, Sir David Attenborough, Dian Fossey, Birute Galdikas, Jacques Cousteau, Steve Irwin, Paul Watson, and Ric O'Barry. The gift was given to me in an ornate wooden box, like a treasure chest, with a lock and all over it were water symbols and the various animals that are special in Baja. It was stunning and the gift was so thoughtful. I told him I felt stupid that the gift I had given him was so inadequate. He laughed, "You're my gift Lily," and so I decided I couldn't and wouldn't compete and let it go.

My Dad gave me a car! He found me an older, slightly beat up pathfinder that was perfect and I loved it. I couldn't believe how well my first Christmas without my Mother actually went, in fact, I felt very guilty about it, but I focused on the family that hadn't abandoned me and my Golden God.

Between Christmas and New Year's Day Emilio and I focused and worked tirelessly on our college applications. I used Emilio's San Diego address for my applications so that when our letters arrived, he could open both of ours together. We applied to several universities along the west coast, with our number one choice being Scripps Institution of Oceanography and we also applied here in La Paz, where they have a great marine biology program. We were hopeful that at least one of these places would accept us both. Emilio would take our applications and mail them from the states upon his return (except for the ones we could apply for online).

We spent New Year's Eve with the Sentinels and a few other friends of Ruby's and some of Catarina's at a party at Fernando's, which happened to have a great view of the ocean and the fireworks. The next morning, we had plans with my Aunt Danni.

She picked us up and said to dress comfortably and bring a hoodie or sweater. Emilio of course was invited along, but it was a family outing, which included the boys, Elena, and even Bilbo. We arrived at the marina in Cabo San Lucas where she told us we were going on a whale watching boat. Whale season had just begun and we might not see whales, Aunt Danni and our captain warned us, but at least it would be a day out on the ocean. We went out, it was a partly cloudy day, a bit cold (for here anyway) and the water was choppy with white caps as far as the eye could see. Our captain said it would be hard to spot whales today with the rough seas, "but they're out there so you never know", he said.

I leaned back against Emilio's chest and let him warm me, the boys were making up some ridiculous song about pirates and making everyone laugh. Those two were always singing and happy, I often wondered how their lives might be different because our Mom left us. They seem unaffected, but they can't be.

I closed my eyes and let the rocking of the boat relax me, while Emilio wrapped his arms around me, my protector, I smiled to myself. Just then I popped up and pointed, "That way", I told the captain.

"I don't see anything", he said, looking at me like a parent looks at their kid who said something funny.

"THAT way!", I practically yelled at him, but not in a rude way, in an excited way, I hope.

He looked at my Dad who nodded and he turned the boat in the direction which I'd pointed. I climbed to the front of the boat, Emilio following me and I closed my eyes and held out my arm in the direction we should go, I shifted it as the whales changed directions and the captain followed my signals. Then I held up a fist, indicating he should stop, which he did. We all sat there quietly, so quietly, as the boat rocked us back and forth, just as the Captain was going to say something, two huge humpback whales breached, their full bodies leaping out of the water and slamming down on the water with force and grace and so much power that we were awestruck. Tears were streaming down my face; they were the most beautiful creatures I'd ever seen. How could they be so giant and so graceful at the same time? I looked back to see the Captain standing there with his mouth open, maybe because the whales were not 10 feet from our boat!

"We can follow them," I shouted at him, bringing him back out of his stupor. The boys were screaming, my Aunt and Catarina were fumbling to pull out their cameras, smiling from ear to ear, and I think my Dad looked like he was going to cry.

"Amazing", Emilio whispered in my ear, "so amazing".

We followed them for hours as they breached and waved at us with their fins, showed us their enormous flukes. I could hear their singing underneath the water and I knew that there were others nearby. It was hard to hold back the tears of joy streaming down my face, but when I turned to look at everyone, they weren't looking at me, so I didn't worry about it and just opened myself up to them.

Other boats saw us and started to follow the whales too, we could hear oohs and ahhhs coming from the other boats, while we too were riveted. They weren't talking to me, they were courting each other and I felt their playfulness and joy. After about two hours of the whale show, they dove deep and we couldn't see them and the quiet returned. They popped up once more, between us and another boat and floated alongside us for just a moment, checking us out. They sent something like "Little Flower, tell your friends to go now". They talked to me! Me! Who else could be Little Flower? Was I making it up in my head because Chavela calls me that? I didn't take a chance. I told the captain we needed to go now, it was a signal I said and I told him to signal the other boats to stop following them now. With that the whales showed us their flukes one last time and dove to the depths they inhabited.

"I've been whale watching many times," my Aunt said, "but it's never been anything like that, they put on a show, just for us, never have I felt connected to them like that." She shook her head in disbelief. The captain was so quiet all the way back, he seemed stunned.

After that I knew, something I hadn't known before, I felt like I was meant to take care of them, speak for them, protect them, I just had to figure out how. That day, Emilio and I went back to my house and started to plan our whale watching trip for February, when he'd be back for ten days. We ran it by my Dad and altered the plan, according to his feedback.

I dropped Emilio at the airport, his family went separately this time. We had decided to stop at the beach for about an hour before he had to leave. I sat between his legs with my back to his chest as we sat and stared out at the ocean. The mobula rays were jumping and flying through the air, a spectacular sight to see, there were hundreds, it was incredible. We sat together not saying a word, spellbound by the rays. I couldn't speak, the thought of him leaving was incredibly hard to face, but the upcoming trip in a month and a half would keep me in good spirits. I would focus on my work and wait to see him again.

...

Catarina and the Bagginses arrived in February for President's break or ski week as it's called on the East Coast. This was not a holiday in Cabo, so Ruby, Fernando, Santi and I had to take some days off. Because we had to make up all our work, we did homework in the car while Catarina and Emilio took turns driving.

The plan was that the Sentinels would go camping at San Ignacio lagoon where we'd go see whales and their babies. Then we'd drive back across to the Gulf side and meet my Dad and the boys and go whale watching in Bahia Concepcion.

We arrived to San Ignacio a bit late and had to set up our camp on the beach in the dark, it was eerie and not the smartest way to do it, but we laughed and fumbled with our tents and figured everything out, but went to bed hungry. One condition my Dad had set was that I share a tent with Catarina and to avoid an awkward conversation, I promised to do so. So we had a girls' tent and a boys' tent and we were so tired from the long drive and the excitement of the trip, we didn't think to disobey orders, we just went to sleep.

In the morning we got up early and had breakfast, though I couldn't really eat, I was too excited. Emilio forced a granola bar and some juice on me and we got ready to go get on the boat. Our panga was the typical boat here, like everywhere in Baja and we were lucky to get one all to ourselves, usually they'll squeeze at least 10-12 people on there. We had no shade on this one so we all grabbed hats and sunscreen, excited and anxious, to see these whales, known to many as "the friendlies".

I didn't have to "help" the captain, he'd been doing this his whole life he told us and really the whales here would come to us, there was no need to go looking. It was the most magnificent day with blue skies and calm waters and the Sentinels were all in significantly good moods. After about a half an hour, we saw our first whale. She came right up to the boat and nudged her newborn calf toward us. Everyone had a chance to reach over and rub the baby on its side and then she turned over, wanting a tummy rub. It was glorious to see these creatures, twice the size of our boat, coming right up next to us and staring at us with it's all knowing eye. I was starting to feel overwhelmed, the mother had so many questions to ask me and I didn't know what to do with all the emotion. Emilio sensed what I was feeling and took my arm and started to massage my hand in way that was so calming, I began to breathe and I tried closing my eyes for a moment. The baby didn't talk to me, it just sent me feelings of joy and newness and wonder, much like the baby turtles, but on a much deeper level. The mother was incredibly curious and wanted to know about us. She wanted to know if we came to see them like they came to see us. She explained that while these were their birthing grounds for hundreds of generations (it was warm and shallow enough that no predators would enter, i.e. orcas) that they now also came to see us and that they would teach their babies about us and that we are all connected. She said that as long as it was safe, they would continue to come here forever. I promised to spread her message among us and to help and keep this area protected for them. It was an indescribably eye-opening experience for all of us and I tried to explain to the captain what the whale said, without him knowing that the whale actually said it or so that he wouldn't think I was a total crazy person. I told the captain that I'd read all this scientific research, but I sensed he wasn't buying my story. He gave me a knowing look and promised to spread the message and I trusted he wouldn't give me up.

We couldn't stop talking about the day and it was hard to unwind and go to bed. I couldn't keep my eyes open, it had been an incredibly draining experience for me. I'm guessing that Emilio put me to bed because I awoke at dawn, in my tent, in my sleeping bag, still in my clothes, but my shoes off and my hair loose. Catarina was next to me and Emilio was curled up behind me, his strong arms around me. I got up quietly so as not to disturb and went out onto the beach and basked in the first light of day. I practiced my meditation and didn't notice Emilio sitting next to me, quietly studying me.

"Good morning beautiful," and he flashed that brilliant smile that melted me every time. "You didn't hear me at all, your meditative trances are getting better."

I gave him my warmest smile and leaned over to kiss him. "I love you". I hopped up and started to wake everyone up so that we could pack up and get on the road, I needed to get to the next whale experience, I was hooked.

Catarina and the rest of the Sentinels headed back to San Jose after dropping Emilio and I with my Dad and the boys at Bahia Concepcion. It would be a crazy day, but it would be worth it. We told my Dad about the previous day as we drove to catch our boat for the day. My Dad and the boys had arrived last night and booked our boat and camped out as well. It was warmer on the gulf side and I didn't think we'd need our hoodies this trip, but we grabbed our gear and got ready to launch. We rode around the bay for about an hour, I was tired and Emilio was busy asking the captain a bunch of questions about being a boat captain, and the boys were getting restless.

"Use your whale magic Lily", Luca said, much too loudly for my comfort.

"Whale magic, whale magic, whale magic," Ollie started chanting.

"Shhhhh, stop that," I blushed, not knowing what to do or say.

Emilio distracted the boys by showing them a length of rope he had and started teaching them how to make knots, I was so relieved. The captain stopped the boat for a bit while he looked out around him, trying to spot whale slicks (whale "footprints") or spouting. I started to feel strange, my hands went clammy and I felt pressure in my chest. Emilio suddenly stopped what he was doing to look up at me and was at my side in a split second. "I cccan't breathe," it came out in a whisper.

"Put up your shield, that place where you go when you're meditating, but leave a window open, so that you are still here with us too. I'm going to count and I need you to inhale slowly as I count to five and then exhale from 6 to 10". He started counting and just as I started to feel out of control, I started to focus on his voice and the feeling started to pass. There was still that heavy pressure on my chest, but I knew it wasn't mine, it belonged to someone else, well not exactly some-one, but some-thing else.

I kept my eyes closed, breathing with Emilio's counting, and I heard him say "she's okay, she's okay", to my Dad I would imagine. I pointed where we needed to go and Emilio told the captain to follow my lead. He did I suppose because I felt us getting closer. When I felt we were just above them, I told Emilio to stop the boat. The captain stopped us and I opened my eyes.

"Dad, I need your help, boys, you too, Emilio, you need to stay in the boat and direct the captain if necessary, he started to shake his head but I insisted. Dad, boys, bring your diving knives and follow me. I jumped in and they followed without question, which was strange, but appreciated.

As we were treading water by the boat I told them to wait a moment and while Emilio was handing them masks, I dove. I saw what I had sensed, there were two whales, a mother and calf, caught in a drifting gill net. The mother was trying desperately to push her baby to the surface to breathe. I swam back up.

"Ready?", I looked at the boys and Dad. They nodded. "There are two whales stuck in a net, we need to take turns diving down and cut it off, we have to be fast, the baby needs to breathe now, so free the baby first. Me and Luca first, watch us from up here and dive down when we are coming up to breathe. Everyone nodded. Little Luca looked at me, fearless, with his knife in his hand as if he was twenty, not six. He was faster than me and got there first, I pulled at the net and he cut as much as he could and then we signaled to go up, on our way up, Ollie and Dad swam down past us. They were able to finish the cuts on the net and free the baby. As Ollie and Dad came up, they pulled as much net as they could with them and we climbed into the boat and started to pull up the net, the mother was able to surface with the net and floated by us while we cut the rest of it off of her. The mother whale's gratitude flooded me with emotion and I broke down for a moment, but it passed quickly, which was a first, maybe I was getting better at this and having Emilio by my side, I felt stable and in control.

The captain pulled in the rest of the netting and promised to be on the lookout for fishermen using nets and other illegal activity that might harm the whales, he was one of us, a sea sentinel for sure. As we headed back to shore I asked the captain to take a slight detour and we were able to see something most humans will never see, the elusive blue whale. It doesn't spend as much time at the surface as other whales and we don't know as much about them, but the sheer size of it was mind boggling, it was the size of a football field! Even though we couldn't see her, his mate was in the depths below and though they didn't speak to me, I could feel their emotions, yes, they definitely feel emotions, and they were happy to be cruising along together and anxious about the impending birth of their calf. We followed until the large male, who I sensed had come to see me, dove to report back to his mate. I could only hope that I got a good report, one of friendship and love.

As we headed back to the dock, the captain, who refused his tip (laughing and saying I should be getting the tip), would only accept money for gas. This was just as much a new experience for him as it was for us. He said he'd never rescued whales before and much less seen a blue whale and he thanked us and asked if I could teach him my whale finding trick. I told him I was just good at spotting them and Emilio distracted him with a handshake and a change in conversation.

My Dad drove us home in silence. Any time I thought he was going to say something, he would just mutter to himself, "Wow," and shake his head. I made my way to the back seat and asked Emilio to take the front passenger seat. I was so tired and I wanted to sleep, like the boys, who had fallen asleep about thirty seconds after the car had started. I knew Emilio would feel obligated to stay awake with my Dad and keep him company on the long drive and I knew I should feel guilty about it, but I was just too tired. I drifted off almost immediately and didn't wake until we were home. It was late and Emilio stayed over, on the couch, and we all awoke to a magnificent breakfast expertly prepared by Elena, who had become a vegetarian herself after her whale experience on New Year's Day.

The last of our February days together were spent in a whale magic stupor. We went to a different beach every day and counted whales, we made the most of every moment until my Golden God left me once more, with the promise to return at spring break.

Chapter 19
Cold in Cabo

Spring break was spent in blissful contentment, watching whales, snorkeling, reading books, exploring, going on hikes, taking photos. Emilio and I luckily had the same week of spring break, though I had two weeks and he had one, and we took advantage of every moment we had together. We spent time with our families, but selfishly we hoarded as much time as we could for each other. We continued our plans and talked about which colleges we thought we'd get into and we dreamed about where we would be a year from now, 10 years from now. We talked about volunteering for Sea Shepherd and helping to stop whaling around the world. We talked about so many things, but we also spent a lot of time not talking, because we didn't need to, our connection was so strong.

We met with the Sentinels and brainstormed missions we could accomplish in the summer and we went out to the clubs and took part in the night life and experienced the "spring break" people see on TV, though the best part of that was people watching.

We met with Chavela at the Mercado and she invited us for dinner at her house. She had set the table beautifully, for six, and we wondered who else would come. "Sit down, sit down," she said and led us to a little corner of the courtyard. I wanted to talk to you for a moment before the others arrive. "I ran in to some old friends in town and I invited them to join us, I hope you don't mind, so we won't be talking about your gifts. I feel your connection growing stronger as you both start to understand your gifts. I invited you here to, to…" and she stopped as though she'd forgotten what she wanted to say or changed her mind about saying it, I couldn't tell which, "to show you my new lilies," and she grabbed my hands over to where she'd planted several varieties of lilies and they were growing as beautifully as the rest of her lush garden.

"Magnificent," I said.

"Just like you," Emilio whispered in my ear. I laughed shaking my head, I wasn't great at taking compliments. I noticed Chavela staring at us as if she knew something we didn't, she smiled and turned.

"The other guests have arrived, help me serve them drinks."

The other guests were a lovely, older French couple and Chavela's sister, Carmen. Carmen was soft spoken and seemingly shy, but so sweet. The French couple were from the French countryside, near the French Alps. We had lovely wine, I never thought I would like wine, but it was good, though I was careful not to have too much. Shy, unassuming Carmen played the most amazing acoustic guitar and sang like an angel, it was a wonderful evening, as expected with Chavela.

Each time I had to leave Emilio became more difficult. This would be our longest separation, but it would hopefully be our last. We promised to focus on graduating and finishing our "to do" lists and enjoying this time in high school as it would soon be gone forever.

April came and went, we spoke as often as we could, but we were both so busy trying to finish school, community service and family obligations. May was here and the graduation festivities would be starting with graduation less than a month away.

I talked to the girls, at least one of them, each day. They were so excited about my early graduation and couldn't believe they still had to do their senior year, without me. I had started to plot with Sophie, that I would come to Emilio's graduation, which was a week after mine. It would be a surprise for him and for the girls. I would stay at Sophie's and we'd convince my Dad to get me a plane ticket as a graduation gift, if not, Sophie would use her savings. The girls kept me in the loop about their lives and boys and parties and everything. I missed Emilio, but I missed my friends too and I'd seen so little of them this year. They were all excited about the annual Wild Coast Baja Gala, which was basically a gala-style fundraising event, but it wasn't formal and we loved going every year. As volunteers, we helped pass out food and helped run the silent auction and we usually got to have fun and dance the night away with the bands they brought, which were always super cool. As a volunteer, Emilio would get to go this year too and his parents would be going as patrons.

I didn't spend as much time in the water as usual, it had been pretty windy and I had so much school work to finish with a quickly approaching deadline. I did spend quite some time with Mrs. Woodpecker who seemed to enjoy flying into my room at all hours. The little bird had a prickly personality and I often honed my gift by "talking" to her. She loved to mess with Bilbo and I have to admit, their entanglements amused me and I frequently let them play without interference. She had informed me that she was my official liaison to the local bird community. Don't ask me how I understood that, but I did. Today though, they were really at each other and I had to scold them both and asked Mrs. Woodpecker to go home.

I received a text from Emilio, with the simple message: Please call me. I was about to when Mrs. Woodpecker came in again, wanting a piece of yarn she'd seen on my carpet. I gave it to her and she flew away again, saying goodnight. I went back to my bed to grab my phone and call Emilio when it started ringing and I noticed it was a FaceTime call from Summi.

"Can't wait to hear about the Gala, how did it go?"

"I need to tell you something." She said almost robotically, she had something in her hands that she was fidgeting with. I sat quietly, waiting for her to open up.

"Emilio and I like each other. Not in the friend way. We LIKE each other." I knew what she meant when she emphasized the "like". I sat in shock. Actual shock, I couldn't speak, I just shook my head, I think I babbled something like "no, that can't be".

"Face it Lily," she said so coldly, without the remotest hint of remorse. And then she showed me what she had in her hands. It was his necklace. The one I gave him, the one I had made for him, the one that symbolized that he was my protector. She unwound it and started to put it around her neck and I hung up the phone. I couldn't watch another moment; I couldn't hear another word. I could not understand what was happening. I curled up on my bed with tears streaming down my face, involuntary tears as I felt numb, it was the shock. My phone kept buzzing and then ringing, but I couldn't, I just couldn't, I turned it off and just lay in my bed shivering, I felt so, so, so cold.

I don't know how I ever fell asleep and I didn't know what time it was when I woke up, with a puffy face and a cold heart, at least I felt so cold inside. I needed my friends, but every time I thought about my friends I thought of Summi, Why, why, why, why, why? I was stuck on a loop. I decided to call Sophie and luckily she picked up right away and Evi was with her.

Before I could even speak, I started to cry. They let me cry and cry and cry until I stopped.

"Summi, she (hiccup, hiccup), I don't understand, I can't, what happened?" I knew I wasn't making any sense, but they sat there in silence.

"We know." Sophie said quietly, "We were there, we made her call you."

I couldn't speak, what did they mean they were there? Were they at her house when she called, sitting, listening to her destroy me? I shook my head.

Evi started to speak but I interrupted her.

"Tell me what you know. I need to know and I need to know now." I saw Evi shaking her head, she looked so angry.

"Yes, Evi, she needs to know," Sophie took a deep breath, "we have nothing to do with this Lily, we love you and well, I'll tell you what happened, we can only tell you what we saw, it's all we know. We were at the Baja Gala and we were having a great time, Emilio was there with his family, we were all dancing, we'd had a couple of beers that we'd snuck in, but nothing major. Evi and I were dancing and we went back to the office to drink the last beer we'd hidden in our bag and when we opened the door, we saw them."

I thought I was going to faint, I don't think I was breathing, but I kept quiet, waiting for the rest.

"Emilio had his back to the desk, leaning against it and his shirt was partially open, and his pants were, I don't know, it was so fast, and Summi had her hand," Sophie was cut off.

"That's enough, that's enough. That's all. We interrupted something that wasn't right, that's all you need to know. We don't really know, but it wasn't right. Emilio pushed her away and looked at us and was about to say something but ran out. We didn't see him again." Eva explained.

"I yelled at her," Sophie said. "And she just stood there, so cold, so matter-of-fact and she said, "What? So we like each other," but before she could walk out we blocked the door. We said that she needed to call you and that if she didn't call you, we would. We were just about to when you called us. I'm so sorry Lily, I'm so sorry, you're going to be okay, I promise".

I was crying hysterically then and I could tell they were worried, I heard them saying they loved me as I hung up the phone. I texted Sophie, "I can't talk right now, call you later, love you, bye."

The sadness overtook me and I went back to my bed and pulled the covers over my head. I'd turned off my phone and just stared at the ceiling as the tears ran down my cheeks. I was relieved that my Dad and the boys were surfing and the house was empty. Bilbo hopped on my bed and tried to nuzzle me. I didn't let him. He refused to get off my bed and just sat at my feet licking my toes. I basically spent two days like this. I pretended I was sick, which I was in a way. My very soul was sick, but I knew I had to get up. I knew I had to go to school and I would pretend, fake it till you make it they always say.

I turned my phone back on. I had so many calls and texts from Emilio, too many to count. I deleted them without reading them, I just didn't want to know. Just then it rang and it was him. It was a regular call, no video. I knew if I saw him,

I would break into a million pieces, but I needed to make him stop, so I answered the call.

"Thank god, Lily, I…". He sounded desperate, I needed to not hear his voice either.

"Don't talk, I'm begging you, don't talk," it was quiet on the other end. "I can't see you or listen to you or communicate with you right now, I just can't, it's too painful. I only ask two things," I thought I heard him say, "anything" but ignored it and continued, "if you ever cared about me, at all, you will NEVER and I mean NEVER see or speak to her again," I couldn't even say her name, "as far as you know, she doesn't exist. Do you understand me? Do you agree to this?"

"I agree, I haven't, never, I promise, I promise". I couldn't stand the sadness in his voice, I thought I would throw up.

"Don't talk!!!!!" I screamed, like a lunatic, a lunatic whose heart had been ripped apart. I didn't care that I'd asked him a question. I needed him not to talk. "And don't call me or text me or anything. I'll contact you when I'm ready." And I hung up, I got dressed and I went to school.

I was a zombie. I couldn't really talk, I didn't want to talk and even though Ruby, Fernando and Santi knew something was wrong, they didn't pry and they just pretended I wasn't a zombie, which I secretly thanked them for. I don't know if people noticed my muteness or if they even noticed a difference, they couldn't see my insides, that's where the wounds were, where the depressive infection had taken hold. I tried to smile when others laughed, I tried to nod when people were looking for my agreement and I made sure not to turn down invitations to do things. I can't imagine how anyone could tolerate my presence in this state, but they kept inviting me.

Any down time was spent in my room, and if no one was home I just cried. The birds took turns "watching" me, I'm not sure what they thought I would do, I was broken, but not suicidal. I almost enjoyed when the robin came, she would nestle in my hair and play with it, like my Mom used to play with my hair until I fell asleep. I almost enjoyed it except when it made me think about my Mom. Sometimes I analyzed and analyzed and then reanalyzed what had happened and sometimes the pain was so overwhelming I'd try to meditate, but it just didn't work. Nothing worked.

At school, I spent every free moment hiding in the greenhouse. Usually Santi would find me and sit down with me in the dirt. He wouldn't talk, he'd just stroke my hand while he read a book or he'd stroke my hair and tell me everything would be all right, but he never asked and he never tried anything and he was very kind, making sure that I ate and he always brought me new books to read. Sometimes I would smile, but mostly I just sat there, staring out at nothing, numb, numb, numb was where I wanted to be, I didn't want to feel anything.

After several hours of homework, I was doing my usual staring at the ceiling, when Elena came in. She sat on my bed and put the back of her hand to my forehead, to see if I had a temperature I suppose. She moved the hair out of my face, I hadn't noticed it, and pinched my cheek. "You're okay, why don't you go to the beach or go watch TV downstairs so I can clean your room?"

"I'll clean it."

"No, go on, I'll," and then she stopped, "okay," and she brought in the broom, mop and duster. She said something else in Spanish I didn't quite catch, something like "cleaning therapy," but I was relieved she left, I just wanted to be alone in my room. I also didn't want her to spend too much time in my room, what if the birds came in when she was here?

I decided to dust first and started with my books and shelves. As I looked around I started to feel dizzy, there were so many photos, of her, of him, so many reminders. First I collected everything that reminded me of him and put it in the carved wooden box he'd given me, including all the books, and I put it and everything else that didn't fit in it, in the closet, tucked away in the back where I never looked. Then I took down every photo I had with her in it and I proceeded to cut her out. If it was just her and I, I ripped in into tiny pieces and threw it in the trash can. If it was with all the girls, I cut her out neatly and put the picture back where it was. I finished cleaning my room, it felt cleansed of her taint, but at the same time, without the reminders of Emilio, it felt empty, and the sadness overtook me once again.

The cleaning therapy had some effect, but I still couldn't erase the fact that it was his 18th birthday today and that if THE BETRAYAL hadn't happened, we'd be celebrating, virtually, but celebrating. I couldn't stand it and decided to go for a walk, yelling to Elena as I walked out the door. Luckily, I could walk to the nearest beach in about 20 minutes, it wasn't my favorite beach, but at this point it didn't matter. I went and sat in the sand until the sun went down. I decided to walk back a different way so I could stop at the grocery store or get some ice cream in the little mall next to it. I decided on a gelato and went to eat it in a little park nearby. The last few kids were being dragged away by their parents as the sunlight faded, leaving only the full moon's bright glow.

I was in a constant state of alternating between sadness and numbness. I'd be so deeply sad and then when it became too much to bear, I'd go numb. But sustaining the numbness proved to be difficult and I'd slip back into the sadness from one minute to the next. That's what happened. I was swinging on the swing, watching the full moon rising, when the sadness seeped back in and in my vulnerable state, I heard them. There was a dolphinarium a block away, completely landlocked, with high cement walls surrounding what I could only imagine was a pool with dolphins in it. I felt so bad for them, walled in, only being able to see the sky above, not knowing they were 300 yards from the ocean, so close, but so far.

I got an idea and went back to the grocery store, it was more of a Walmart type store that didn't just have food, but many household items as well. I found some paint and brushes and headed out, determined. Along the outer walls of the dolphinarium there were large blown up pictures of seemingly happy dolphins beckoning people to come in and swim with them. It was disgusting and a wave of nausea overtook me. After I'd wretched in the bushes, I opened a can of paint and started to change the pictures. I painted the dolphins' mouths, extending them downward to look like sad faces. I painted tears, blood red, coming out of their eyes. Over one dolphin I painted a thought bubble saying, "Help me". As I went to paint another thought bubble I heard them talking.

"Who is out there, what's happening, come here, come here," they called. I left the paint can and brush and walked around the place, trying to find a way in. "He's not here, come in, come in." I walked around to the front entrance, it was closed, but there was a main door. I looked around and found a bucket behind the reception desk and stood up on it and hauled myself up over the door. I fell to the other side, it hurt, I might have sprained my wrist, but that type of pain didn't faze me. I just cradled my wrist and walked toward the dolphin pool. It was just a big pool, about the size of a competitive swimming pool. It was incredibly sad. Since I was so sad, I just wanted to commiserate and sit with the dolphins and feel sad together. I sat at the deeper end of the pool with my legs in the water. They came up to me and wanted to talk, but noticed quickly I didn't feel like talking. They felt my pain and nudged me and floated near me so I could pet them and connect with them I suppose. I couldn't tell anymore if I was feeling their sadness or they were feeling mine, but if they could cry, they would have, I could feel them.

My mind had drifted into nothingness, almost as if I was asleep, when I was suddenly jerked awake. "Someone's coming, someone's coming, they're coming for you, go, quickly, hurry, oh no, oh no," they screamed in my head, those sad dolphin voices. I let the thought creep into my mind again, am I crazy?

And suddenly I heard the commotion and saw five police officers running toward me, two running around one side of the pool and three running around the other side, there was nowhere for me to go. I pulled out my phone, texted my Dad "911" and pinned my location, it took only seconds. I then stuffed the phone down the front of my denim shorts and threw my hands up in surrender. I didn't know if I was surrendering to the police, or to my pain, I was in a daze.

The police were grabbing me and shouting questions at me and I just stood there, unresponsive. I think they couldn't understand why I wasn't saying anything. I heard them say something to each other about "she must not understand

Spanish," another said, "no, I think there's something wrong with her". I just stood there, staring at nothing, unable to speak, unwilling to speak, I couldn't tell, I just knew that no words would be coming out of my mouth. I could sense commotion behind me as the desperate dolphins swam around, wanting to help me, but unable to do so. I could sense frustration and worry coming from them. As the police grabbed my arms and started hauling me out of there, I sent them a message.

"I'm so sorry, I don't know how to help you, but I will find a way, I promise".

I was standing up against the police truck as they were having a discussion when my Dad arrived, running toward me, distraught, he hugged me, but I just stood there in silence. He looked me over to see if I was hurt, I still cradled my wrist, but he decided I was okay and went to talk to the police. They sounded like they were far away, but they were just a few feet away. I could see my Dad take his card out of his pocket and hand it to them, I also saw him pull out some money, at least that's what I thought. I felt like I was behind an invisible force-field that blurred everything that was happening. It seemed like an eternity and I was so tired. My knees gave out at that point and I slid slowly to the ground and just sat, waiting.

Eventually, my Dad came over and helped me up and over to the car. I couldn't tell if he was mad or not, as we drove away, he looked at the "paint job" I'd given the front of the dolphinarium and started laughing. I looked at him, he just kept laughing and laughing, soon, I was laughing too.

Chapter 20
Avancer

Graduation day was here and I couldn't believe it was actually happening. My high school experience had started out as quite typical, at a huge school, with sports and lockers, cliques and prom queens, everything that Hollywood said it would be. Then my world was turned upside down and I moved to this quiet little school, with a greenhouse, grades K-12 and a graduating class of nine students that I barely knew (I had done so many classes as independent study). Luckily I didn't care about that. Ruby, Fernando, and Santi were there of course and my Dad and brothers. My Aunt was away at Catarina's graduation, but she called to congratulate me early this morning. I tried not to think about it, but there it was, nagging at me, annoyingly, the thought that my Mother was not here to see me graduate from High School, not because she couldn't, but because she chose not to. I focused on those who were there, willingly.

We had a nice dinner with my friends and family and Chavela attended, which was such a wonderful surprise. I was careful not to sit next to her, I didn't want to have to talk about Emilio and I just knew she would have questions. Maybe she sensed my desperation, if that's what it was, because she only had well wishes and congratulations for me, no questions or intrusions. We laughed and ate and somehow I avoided all the questions about my future and what college I'd be attending. I knew that I would have to face that part of life soon, but I wasn't ready, and all of my college letters would be at Emilio's house, I dared to wonder, for just a moment, if he'd opened them.

I told the Sentinels what I had done to the dolphinarium. They weren't too pleased. First of all because I got caught, second because they worried they'd link me to the sticker campaign, and third because if the police remembered me, I'd be a target of theirs, forever. They did laugh about it though and we joked about how I would have to shave my head and get a bunch of tattoos to change my appearance.

Sophie and Eva called, they had wanted to be here but it was finals week for them and they couldn't come. They avoided THE subject and filled me in on their recent outings and activities, none of which seemed to include Summer. Eva would be away all summer playing with the Under 17 National Team, which was pretty amazing and Sophie would be working with the Junior Lifeguard program, helping teach and supervise all the groms. To think that we were the groms not too long ago.

After hanging up, I stopped for a moment to think of what my life would be like right now if my Mom hadn't left. I'd have a Mom, so that's a big deal, though I'm often angry at her I still miss her every day. I would still be in San Diego, studying for finals and getting excited for Senior year. I would not have met Chavela, so I'd probably be seeing a therapist, who'd agree that I was crazy and give me pills. I would not have met HIM and so I'd be pain free and it would still be the fab four instead of the three musketeers. I wouldn't be in Cabo, I wouldn't have freed the dolphins and I wouldn't have experienced whale magic.

I talked to my Dad that night, we hadn't talked like this in a while. I explained that I didn't know where I wanted to go to school yet and that I was thinking of deferring my admission, maybe take the first semester off and start in January. I needed some time, I couldn't explain it, I just needed some time. I told him I really wanted to help at Wild Coast, continue working with the turtle nesting project and maybe develop a new project of my own. My Dad was working a lot right now with a group of citizens, trying to fight a huge thousand-acre development near Cabo Pulmo. A foreign company wants to build a huge resort on undeveloped land that is right next to the marine reserve, one of the largest reefs in all of Mexico. It would be ruined with so many people, construction, pollutants, etc. He's trying to use the courts to fight the development and it's become his major focus, though he still helps Wild Coast, the Mercado Organico, and the farm.

He was supportive of my decision to delay my admission and he didn't mention my brush with the law, but I brought it up. "Thank you for saving me Dad, another stupid decision on my part."

"Your heart was in the right place Sweets, those places are disgusting. They're on my list, once I protect Cabo Pulmo, maybe we can focus on shutting those places down, together."

I nodded and hugged him before going up to my room. I threw open the French doors to my balcony to let in some fresh air. Mr. and Mrs. Woodpecker weren't around, but there was a crow perched on the tree and he flew to me as soon as I stepped onto the balcony. He just stared at me, so quiet, what could he be thinking?

"I'm thinking you should water those flowers, they're wilting, like you, you need water too", and with that he flew away.

I looked over at the lilies and they were in fact wilted and actually looked droopy and sad. Did I look like that? I looked in the mirror and I just looked like myself. Maybe that's what I look like on the inside.

…

After the graduation buzz had worn off and a few days had passed, I was contemplating what I should do next, when I heard my Dad coming up the stairs. I was sitting on my bed, with a book and a little wren on my knee and Bilbo by my other knee staring sleepily at the bird. When I heard him heading toward my room, I quickly sent the bird away and sat up.

"What's up Dad?"

"Well, I have an interesting proposition for you. Now I don't want you to overthink it, just take the opportunity and run with it."

I looked at him with a raised brow and what must have been a quizzical look. Was this some sort of trap? "Well what is it?"

"It's a plane ticket, one way, but don't think I'm sending you away, I'll just book the return when you tell me to."

A plane ticket? To San Diego? To be with the girls? I started to get excited. He handed me the envelope and I opened it up. Paris. Paris???? "Dad, what's this, I mean, Paris, why Paris, you want me to go by myself?"

"Slow down, I don't want you to get too excited, but I found your grandmother. Your maternal grandmother lives in Paris and she's invited you to come and stay with her for the summer. Before you say anything, I want you to know that I didn't look for her before because she and your mother are estranged and your mother forbade contact with either of our families and I only met her a couple of times, before they moved back to France, she's not the warmest person, but she's your grandmother and this is an opportunity that may never come up again."

It was a lot to take in. I have a grandmother? "Do I have other family I don't know about?"

"Your mom has a sister and two brothers, they might have children, so there's a possibility of cousins too."

I sat in silence for a minute, with a million thoughts running through my head, I glanced back down at the ticket. "Wait, this is for three days from now, I leave in three days?!?"

My Dad was smiling, "Yes, you leave in three days and you will love it."

I was going to Paris. I recognized the departure date because it was the day Emilio was graduating and I'd been planning to go to San Diego and surprise him. But the surprise was on me. I'm going to Paris.

"You'll fly to LA and catch your Paris flight there, it's direct, and someone will pick you up at the airport in Paris. It's all arranged. I knew you wouldn't pass this up. I would go with you but your grandmother doesn't like me very much and I have so much to do here. You go meet her and next time we can take your brothers. I'll bring up your suitcase, you can start planning what to pack."

He left and I called the girls on my laptop. While I talked to them, we researched the weather and what I should bring and what I should just buy there. I knew my wardrobe would not exactly be Parisian fashion, but I'd just make do with what I had and not worry about that. The girls were so excited and jealous too, but in a good way, and we stayed up talking late, until they finally had to go to bed because of school the next day.

I had breakfast with the family that morning, Elena had out done herself with the most amazing chilaquiles and fresh squeezed grapefruit juice I'd ever had. In San Diego they have pretty good Mexican food, in fact they have pretty good Mexican vegetarian food, but nothing compares to this woman's cooking. She is a master. One of my favorite meals she makes (besides this one) is potato tacos, she's been experimenting with a sweet potato version with my Dad's crop and they are so delicious. We talked about how I was going to make it in France as a vegetarian. My Dad promised it was possible and that it was a good thing I ate dairy, because their cheese is world famous. He also said that though he didn't have a very long conversation with my grandmother, he did remind her I am strictly vegetarian and she said she would do her best to accommodate me in that aspect, whatever that means.

I was going to miss the boys and they were already asking me to bring them soccer shirts and fighting over which ones they wanted. I couldn't believe they were six years old. They definitely looked six, but they seemed so much older in so many ways.

"Are you sure I can't take Bilbo?" I asked again. My Dad had a list of reasons why I couldn't but I didn't want to go alone and Bilbo was such a good companion. The boys laughed and said that they were going to take care of him and Bilbo just stared up at me, begging to come with me. I stared back and told him that he would have to stay and take care of the boys while I was away. Bilbo was happy to have a job and promised to stay with them until I came back.

I left the wilted lilies with my Aunt. I asked her to please take them to Chavela, she would be able to bring them back to life, they used to be so beautiful. Chavela left me a message on my phone, I'd missed her call, "Things are not always what them seem, you will heal, keep up your meditation practice. We will have much to discuss when you get home."

Dad and the boys drove me to the airport. It was kind of early, but I had to take a flight that would get me to LA with enough time to catch my Paris flight. We drove, not speaking, with the Beatles playing loudly. When we arrived, Dad offered to park and take me in and take me all the way until we reached security and he could not accompany me further, but I insisted he leave me curbside at departures. It made good bye harder, I told him and I flashed him the Puss in Boots eyes and he agreed. He got out and grabbed my suitcase and the boys stayed in the car. He hugged me and went over all the instructions for the millionth time. As I rolled my suitcase I heard the boys yell at me and hanging out of the window Luca sang "All you need is love" and Ollie chimed in "pa pa ra ra ra" trying to sound like a trumpet, I could hear the song behind them. I laughed and as I turned, I could hear them singing and fighting because one of them shoved the other one and then my Dad yelling "back in your seats," as they drove away.

Dragging my slightly too large suitcase, I checked in on my own, feeling like an adult, sort of, and I headed toward security, but decided to see if they had snacks in the little store first, to take something with me.

Coming out of the store I saw something out of the corner of my eye and had to do a double take. It was Emilio! He was descending the escalator from the arrivals gate, just where I was heading to ascend to the security line. I didn't know what to do. I hid behind a pillar where a family was standing and tried to blend in with them, hide, and look to see where he was so I could run in the opposite direction. As he got to the bottom floor where I was, I saw him trying to get a hold of all his luggage, he had a lot of it, what was going on, what was he doing here, he was supposed to be at his graduation ceremony right now. As he moved toward the exit doors, I moved with the family and onto the escalator without detection. I tried to watch him from behind a lady who had an enormous hat and bags full of souvenirs. He stopped suddenly and turned around, looking around, desperately searching and eventually zeroing in on the escalator, but he couldn't see me, I made sure of it. As he turned again I reached the top, tripping and falling over, almost getting stuck. I crawled away on hands and knees in case I'd caused a commotion and he was looking in my direction again. I could feel him, even though I couldn't see him. I felt a pull, like my body wanted to go one way and my soul another. I crawled along like an idiot until I was sure I was out of sight, everyone must have thought I was just clumsy, with a brace on my wrist and scraped knees. I ran to security and asked people if I could cut in front of them because I was going to miss my flight. I refused to look back. If I looked back, if I saw him, I couldn't trust myself not to run straight to him. I tried to focus straight ahead and strengthened my wobbly knees. I knew if he saw me and called out my name I would, well I don't know what I would do, but I knew I had to choose. Go back or go forward. I just looked forward as I went through security. I prayed that he wouldn't see me or call my name because I wasn't sure I was strong enough to ignore him.

I don't know if he saw me, I don't think he did, though it was strange how he looked around as though searching, for something. Why would it be me, he couldn't know I was here? I went straight to my gate but then thought he might come looking or maybe he was going somewhere and we'd bump into each other, I was so confused, and slightly paranoid. I decided to hide in the bathroom until my flight was boarding. I sat in a stall, meditating, trying not to cry, trying not to dump everything and run out and find him. I quieted my mind as much as I could and then went to board when my flight number was called, trying to breathe deeply.

I was restless and worried, but only up until the plane took off. Once we were off the ground I decided to focus on what lay ahead of me, Paris, Paris, Paris, Paris, I whispered to myself with a smile.

END OF BOOK ONE

"We do not need magic to change the world, we carry all the power we need inside ourselves already: we have the power to imagine better." - J.K. Rowling

"What you do makes a difference, and you have to decide what kind of difference you want to make." - Jane Goodall

"Normal is not something to aspire to, it's something to get away from." - Jodie Foster

Made in the USA
Thornton, CO
05/13/22 22:41:44

3715e3ce-0099-40c1-8b98-fdd96c4d1760R01